My Name Is America

The Journal of
Jasper Jonathan Pierce

A Pilgrim Boy

BY ANN RINALDI

Scholastic Inc. New York

Mayflower
1620

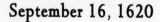

September 16, 1620

When this ship slipped her hawsers and sailed from Plymouth on September 6, I left my brother Tom behind on the wharf. Tom, the other part of me. The younger, yet the wiser. On the streets of London it was Tom who kept us alive. Tom who learned how to beg or steal food. How to stay warm. How to find work, and when we could not, how to pick pockets.

How can I live without Tom? How to go across an ocean and mayhap never see him again? There he stood on the quay, tears coming down his face, he who never cried, not even when our father had died in prison. Not even when there was no money left and we had to take our places with the other orphans on the streets of London.

Tom turned his head for one final look, even as Mr. Blossom, his master, dragged him away. "Meat for the fishes," Mr. Blossom said of us on the *Mayflower*. He and nineteen others on the *Speedwell*, our companion ship, had decided not to go to America after all. Three hundred miles out, the *Speedwell* had started leaking and we went back to port with her for the second time.

I remember standing there as some of her passengers came aboard the *Mayflower.* I looked for Tom. Then the ship weighed anchor and began moving. I ran about, yelling "No, no, you can't go yet, my brother isn't aboard!"

The seaman laughed and pointed to the quay. I ran, tripping over boxes and ropes, to my master. I found him talking to Captain Jones. "My brother! He's left behind! I'm alone!"

My master, Elder Brewster, looked at me with a solemn face. He is not a young man. He is fifty-three. If he was left alone with his Bible for the rest of his life, he would be happy. Yet he had pushed for this trip. "We are all alone, lad," he said, "but for the spirit of God that sustains us. The tide runs out. We have a prosperous wind. There is no going back."

Only a few miles out some were sickened again, though the weather was fair. There they were, puking over the sides. I was ailing too, not from the sea, but from losing Tom. They all envied me, said I was a strong lad, a well-salted lad. They did not know that inside I was dying.

　━　～　～　～

September 17

My full name is Jasper Jonathan Pierce. People will say I do not deserve to use a middle name, because only those of the upper classes have that right. But I use it because my father told me to. "Someday you and your brother will be as good or better than the gentry," he told us. "So use the full name. Even if only for yourself."

For ten days I have languished without my brother. Being accustomed to not eating at all some days on London's streets, many a day on the ship I took naught but a morsel.

"The Saints have finally lived up to their name of puke-stockings," a bound servant named Edward Dotey said. He and Edward Leister belong to Stephen Hopkins, lately of Wotton-under-Edge in Gloucestershire. Hopkins' wife Elizabeth is his second. She has care of Giles, Constance, and Damaris from his first marriage. Constance is my age and most saucy and pretty. Mrs. Hopkins is soon expected to deliver another.

Mr. Hopkins and family are not Saints but Strangers. The Saints are Separatists, the ones who devised this journey. They go to the New World to practice their religion as they wish. It is their desire to be rid of the strong hand of King James, whose reign is a shambles. That's what my father used to say. The others, including myself, are

Church of England. They call us Strangers. Before he was taken to prison, my father had notions of becoming a Saint. He spoke of it often.

The Saints all look after each other. Because my mistress took ill, Mrs. Bradford now cares for me. Today she made broth on her hearth box. We passengers are forbidden to use the ship's galley. Mrs. Bradford is young, some say but eighteen. I made bold to ask her why her spirit was cast down. "Have you left anyone on the dock?" I asked.

She said she and her husband have left a son, name of John, with friends in London. And she mourns for him. I told her about Tom. She gave me this small book and told me to write in it for my brother Tom. I like Mrs. Bradford. Of course she doesn't have the dignity of my mistress. "She was a Simkinson," people say of Mistress Brewster. I think they were gentry.

September 18

We are packed to the gunwales with 102 passengers. I have found a place to sleep, with Dotey and Leister in the shallop. They are about sixteen or seventeen years of age. They tease me because I can write. "He is to be watched," they say. Back in England anyone who is not gentry and who can read and write is considered dangerous. I think they envy my learning, though I told them my brother and I were tutored by a clergyman who'd come to our home. Dotey and Leister are taken with discontents and murmurings. They say their master has been to America before. On his trip to Virginia his ship was wrecked near Bermuda. He told the captain that since he had contracted to serve in Virginia he no longer had to take orders. He was near hanged for it. Now he's a man of considerable means.

September 19

Betimes I look at the blank pages of this book and wonder what I will write. They hold my future. If only I could see it.

September 20

The wind still blows fair. I have taken to hiding away in the shallop during the day when my master does not need my services. It is a good place to write, listen, and watch since it is stowed in the 'tween deck. The top planks on either side have been removed. Before, it was too big to stow even though the *Mayflower* is nine-score, which means 180 tons.

Today I heard one seaman say it is too late in the season for an Atlantic crossing. Another seaman said the fair weather will not last, that cold winds are due down from the Arctic and soon we'll be battling storms.

So I am fain to write now how I come to be on my way to America, a land full of savage beasts in the forest and even more savage men called Indians waiting to kill us if we do not first become meat for the fishes. The rest of this book will be for my brother Tom.

Tom and I were snatched from the streets of London last summer by Mr. Weston, an ironmonger and a man of many schemes, both legal and illegal, they say. Tom and I had done nothing wrong, unless you count the shillings Tom took from the pocket of a gallant. We were attending the hanging of a man who'd been caught killing crows for his supper. It is a public offense to kill crows in London. They alone scavenge dead things off the streets.

"Have you two nothing better to do than pick pockets and watch a man hang?" Mr. Weston asked. We told him we had already earned a few pence that day by running errands for the actors in a nearby theater. That afternoon we meant to go to Paris Gardens to watch a Russian bear fight a brace of mastiffs. He asked us where our mother and father were, as he intended to see us punished. We told him our mother had died of the pox and our father wasted away in prison.

"Ah," he said, "a thief begets thieves."

"Our father was thrown in the clink for harboring

some puke-stockings who were sneaking out of the country without permission of the king," Tom told him. "There he died with not so much as straw between him and the cold floor. Our father was a godly man, a clockmaker. But the king seized his shop and our home for taxes and so we were left to the streets."

I must lay my quill aside now and write more later. It is time to eat.

Later: On the same day we met Mr. Weston, he took us back to his lodgings in the Aldgate section, a poor part of town, but he wasn't tarrying long in London. His clerk fed us. Pea soup. Plum duff. We ate, fair starved. Then he soon told us what he was about: "I act as a backer for a group of Separatists," he said. "Sober, industrious Christians now in Holland. I and some London friends are putting up several thousand pounds to back a plantation for them in North America. They are in need of servants. You could be put to them for seven years, then given your freedom, to stay in America or return to England."

I though Tom would choke on the raisins in his plum duff. "That's halfway across the world!"

"Ships go there every year seeking furs or fish," Mr. Weston said. He told us how the London Company already had a plantation there in Virginia. And how these Separatists would live in the Northern part of the

Virginia plantation, mayhap at the mouth of the Hudson River.

"To what end?" I asked.

"To practice their religion without persecution."

"They are puke-stockings," Tom said. "Psalm-singers."

"If you don't go," Mr. Weston announced, "you and your brother will rot in jail for pickpocketing. And which do you think your father, who harbored these same puke-stockings, would have you do?"

My master calls. I must go.

Later: I write by the light of a small candle on the shallop. When asked, Tom and I both knew what our father would want. Hadn't he told us that the king ran a court of excess? That palace banquets turned into food fights while the poor died of starvation? That someday there would be a place where kings were not considered divine, and when it came to be that we should go there?

So we traveled with Mr. Weston to Leyden in Holland. Tom went to the house of Mr. Blossom, a church deacon. And I to Mr. Brewster. He had gone to Cambridge, and served at Court. Now he labored in a garret with a printer running the Pilgrim Press. They produced tracts that made him a fugitive from the king. He was kind, but absent-minded. He had sons and daughters. I helped in the printer's shop when I did not go to school. Betimes he'd share bread and cheese with me in the shop and tell me of the old days in Scrooby Manor, which was halfway between London and the Scottish border. There he and his friends formed a congregation that broke away from the old ways of worship. When the king struck, terror swept the countryside and a flight to the Netherlands was planned.

He told me of it all in a quiet, modest voice. "Our daughter, born then. We called her Fear. I do not share this with my younger sons, Jasper. They know only happiness and freedom. I share with you."

I listened to the sharing. I spoke of it to no one. It bound me to him in another way.

September 21

One night in Leyden, my master woke me and said he and I were off to London. I asked no questions, but packed hastily. By then I would have followed this gentle, learned, and brave man into hell. As we fled he told me how the king was hunting him, likely to hang him. He and Mr. Brewer, the printer, had made a book the king did not like. They had packed it into French wine vats to smuggle into Scotland.

He did not ask his oldest son Jonathan to go. He asked me. "You know the streets of London," he said. "You know how to hide."

We hid under the king's nose in London. We shared food in garrets. We traveled by night. It was the best time of my life, and I was not afraid. No king could find us. No king did. I have something with my master now that he does not have even with his sons.

September 22

I now write for Tom. Today, Mrs. Bradford begged that I seek out Captain Jones, and ask him to stop his men from mocking the passengers who suffer from seasickness. "Especially that one brutish seaman who mocks Mrs. Hopkins. She has been so ill, and her with child," she said.

I am the one for the task, since there is little to do aboard ship and my master has allowed Cook to borrow me on occasion. This day Cook called me to the forecastle on the upper deck, and gave me a hot caudle to take to the captain. I found Captain Jones poring over his charts.

Here was a man to be reckoned with. He had two wives, six children. He had built his own ship at age eighteen. He did not pray, but neither did he swear. He knew only one order in life. That of the sea. "Know the sea and you will survive anything on land," he told me once when I'd brought victuals to his cabin. Short and squat, he appeared to be ten feet tall when he barked out orders to his men. No one questioned his word. He has been master of the *Mayflower* for eleven years. On my last visit he told me the trip is 2,800 miles. "It's the first time she carries human cargo," he told me. "We'll see. We'll see." He reached for the hot caudle. "The trip should take sixty-six days," he said. I did not reply. I was not expected to, though I wanted to ask him which route he would take. Everyone conjectures about it.

Will it be the southern route, down to the Canaries on the north-east trade winds, then pick up the south-east trades? Or the northern route, circling to Newfoundland then down the American coast? Mayhap he will say southwest to the Azores, on the same latitude as Cape Cod, then west. He will tell no one, certainly not me.

This day I tried to tell him about the brutish seaman plaguing Mrs. Hopkins, but he would not give an ear to me about the matter. "She'll make up to six points on the wind." And I knew he was not talking about Mrs. Hopkins, but his ship, so I said, "Yes sir," and left.

When I told Mrs. Bradford what happened, Mrs. Hopkins was listening. She smiled at me and said, "God will smite the seaman in his own time." You won't believe what happened next, Tom. Within two days this same seaman took grievous ill. He lay in his berth raving and cursing. Giles Heale, the ship's doctor, and Doctor Fuller attended him. They said he had delirium tremens. He died in two more days. The other seamen soon gave up their taunting. Seamen are a suspicious lot, Tom. They think now that the Saints have special powers. I think Mrs. Hopkins has them. Do you know how King James is always wanting to burn women for being witches? I think that if Mrs. Hopkins stayed in London he would soon burn her.

September 23

We have two dogs aboard. One is a mastiff and the other a spaniel. Mr. Goodman has brought them. They run the decks and play. I have made friends with the spaniel.

September 24

Tom, the ocean goes on forever. It is so strange to look and see nothing but water. It is frightening. Will it never end? What am I doing here? Where does this ship take me? Will I ever see you again? I look over the railing and think how deep the ocean is and feel so small and unworthy. The world moves under me, Tom. It moves under us all.

September 25

Do you recollect how Reverend Hornby, our tutor, told us to first write down the facts when we are trying to solve a dilemma? Well, if being aboard this ship on my way to a wild land without you is not a dilemma, I don't know what is. So here are some facts. The crew is fed better than the passengers, even the wealthy ones. The seamen get two pieces of beef on meat days, four pounds of bread, a pint and a half of peas, and four gallons of beer. They may also help themselves to fish, cheese, oatmeal, or water gruel.

There are eighteen servants on board. Most belong to the Leyden Saints. Of the Strangers, only three bring bond servants. Dotey and Leister, two of these, are as full of gossip as fishwives. They both have eyes for Constance Hopkins. They told me that Elder Bradford's heart is back in England with another lass. She refused to wed him and so he wed Dorothy May.

More facts. We have some goats, pigs, and chickens, but no cows. My master has brought many books and plans to set up a school on board. He wears sad-colored clothes most of the time, but on the Sabbath puts on a red vest with silver buttons, just like he did in Leyden. Also a violet cloak, and a blue hat with a broad brim.

I have also made friends with John Alden. He is

twenty, a cooper, a Stranger, and a man of plain common sense. He must test the contents of the barrels of water and beer on board at regular intervals. He asked how I came to know so much about a ship. I told him how you and I often took refuge in the cellar of a ship's chandler on Tower Street, how he let us sleep there amid the canvas, cordage, barrels of pitch, tar, candles, oil, and anchors. "And where did you sleep when the weather was fair?" Alden asked. I told him on the streets. He gave me a queer look and then offered me a taste of the beer. He told me he has an eye for eighteen-year-old Priscilla Mullins. He calls her a comely lass. Her father makes shoes and boots.

Mr. Warren has left his wife and five daughters. Francis Cook left his wife and daughters, but brought his son. My master left two young daughters in the care of their older brother. Degory Priest left his wife and children. And there are others. The wind, this afternoon, grows cold. Mrs. Bradford is making me a jacket. I think I shall go and see if it is finished.

September 26

My jacket is finished and I am most warm and grateful to Mrs. Bradford. My mistress is still sickly. I hope she recovers soon.

October 27

I have not been able to write for weeks. We near lost the ship. I am now sitting belowdecks in a corner behind some barrels, shivering in damp clothing. The passengers are still mopping up, wringing out clothing, and setting everything to rights. We all suffer the ills of confinement, even the dogs. We argue and debate. The young indentured men play cards to the chagrin of the Saints. I have time now to write of the terrible storm.

When the first of it came the sea looked like a mad dog, foaming at the mouth. Tom, you should have heard the boatswain's mate swearing at the seamen to lash the sails. I could not believe how they held themselves so high up there in the shrouds with the ship tossing about. I would like to have watched, but Captain Jones ordered us all below. I helped bolt the portholes on the gun decks. Women were moaning and babies crying. Everything that wasn't tied down flew about, and Elder Bradford set the young men to do the tying. Then the worst came.

The ship shuddered every time a wave poured over the decks. It was dark as night outside, though still mid-afternoon. Lanterns went out and we scrambled about trying to light them, tripping over one another, banging heads. Water poured down the sides and onto berths and clothing. The ship groaned like it would break in half. The

Saints, women and men, were praying, and in the lightning flashes I saw some Strangers praying, too. I never heard the likes of the roaring wind. It was like a thing alive. "We sink! We sink!" Mrs. Bradford yelled. "I will never see my boy again!" Above us we heard seamen's footsteps and shouts from the captain.

Soon the ship was taking on more water. Stephen Hopkins said this was worse than the gale that wrecked his ship on his voyage to Virginia. Then a great splintering sound. They called for the ship's carpenter, and in a short time he told us that a main beam had given way.

John Alden and some of the stronger young men tried to put it back in place, but couldn't. It was terrible. John Alden was swearing, women were praying, men were holding lanterns, giving orders, arguing. There was general mayhem all around. Then my master remembered the great iron screw they had brought from Holland to raise houses in the New World.

Someone argued that if it should break, how would we raise houses in the New World? My master said if we don't reach the New World there would be no need to raise houses. So the screw was fetched. I helped by pushing aside barrels and boxes while the men put it under the cracked beam and screwed it into place. I can write no more now. My mistress calls.

October 28

More about the storm. The screw held and we came through it. Now we eat cold food, sleep in wet beds. Children cough and wail. Both Saints and Strangers say we should turn back. A great deal of debate ensues. Elder Bradford reminded them that if we turn back now, our contract with our backers is broken. And they might never give another for the New World. Someone else said it is as long a way back as the journey ahead. I lay down my quill with their rumbling arguments in my ears, wondering why the backers of this voyage are called the Merchant Adventurers when they are safe at home in dry beds.

October 29

When morning was come, Elder Bradford and Mr. Carver went to Captain Jones to suggest we make for the nearest land, the Canary Islands or Africa. The captain told them the ship was still seaworthy. "I've been with her in storms before. Once we had to throw over half the cargo, but we got through," he told them.

The biscuits are moldy, the butter is rancid, things crawl in all our food. If I must eat any more salt fish I shall perish. John Alden says the beer is going sour. The wind still roars. The captain still keeps us belowdecks and the young men get restless. John Howland, who is bound to John Carver, said he was going on deck. Several advised against it. Howland said Captain Jones was not a king and hadn't we run from kings? To this no reply was given, so Howland opened the hatch grate and climbed onto deck. "Oh, the air!" we heard him bellow.

Then came a new blast of wind, and cries of "Man overboard!" Saint and Stranger men alike climbed onto the deck. The ship was near on its side. Mrs. Bradford hit her head on a supporting beam. We could hear the shouts of the seamen, the barked orders. They say Howland grabbed a rope and was hauled aboard. They brought him down, coughing water, white as death. He lie abed.

October 30

Mrs. Hopkins had her baby. My mistress and other women attended her. The storm still plagued us and we listened to its moans in between the moans of Mrs. Hopkins. My master led prayers for her. I was holding the Hopkins' three-year-old girl, Damaris. And though I am not a Saint and my master never forces me to take part in their devotions, I knelt with them.

Then she was crying out. What was saying?

We stopped praying to listen. "Archangels!" she yelled. "Archangels! I can see from my porthole. They guide our ship!"

No one said a word. Then Mrs. Mullins, mother of the pretty Priscilla, murmured, "She is delirious, poor thing."

"Archangels!" came the cry again. "Look! They will see us safely to the New World!"

I looked out the porthole, but saw no angels. After a long while my mistress came out of the curtained area holding a squalling baby boy. He looked strong and well. Everyone was cheered. Mr. Hopkins said they will name him Oceanus. There was something about the birth that made all feel God had not deserted us and we will get to the New World after all.

"Another brat to care for," I heard Dotey tell Leister later.

November 4

Oh, how I long for a fire! For hot food! Tom, I hope you are eating today a good piece of mutton, wheat flour bread, and a spot of goose liver. I hope you have some green things and some fruit. Because we now have only moldy salt fish and meat. No woman has cooked on her hearth box for weeks. Betimes we smell what the cook is making in the ship's galley and it drives us near mad. I hear rats scurrying behind the ship's beams, trying to get out. I would like a tankard of milk. I do wish we had brought a cow.

November 6

We are ten weeks at sea. Was there ever land beneath my feet? Betimes I think my life with you in London was a dream. And our life before, with our father in our own house, must have been our time in heaven, Tom. A bound servant of Doctor Fuller's took to his bunk and died this day. He was but two and twenty. They are saying it is our first case of scurvy. He was sewn into a canvas shroud, prayed over, and dropped into the sea.

Mrs. Brewster came to me after. "Are you taking your bit of lemon juice each day?" she asked. I said no. "You must," she said. "Or you too will get the scurvy. Two women and some men are complaining of swollen legs, a sure sign."

November 7

Day after tomorrow is my birthday, Tom. I will be fourteen to your twelve. The captain has ordered everyone on deck to exercise. The air is fresh and clear. Before going on deck, however, my master bade me to make myself presentable. He then took me to the Chart Room as a special birthday gift. There is rumor the storm had blown us hundreds of miles off course. Captain Jones showed us the charts. "We are right back on the 42nd parallel," he said. "We should sight land soon." My master asked how soon. Captain Jones scowled, then ventured to say, "Within the week. But I cannot hoist too much sail. The ship is weakened."

Outside again my master let me watch Captain Miles Standish drill his men. He is a man of arms, a soldier of fortune who fought in the Dutch wars. He is sturdy and of no religious persuasion, but has great respect for the Saints. This day he had his men practice loading their matchlocks. They are over five feet long and very heavy. Firing them is a cumbersome business, but when they all fired at once, the very deck shook. How exciting, Tom! Elder Brewster told me we depend on these men to defend us against the savages.

Now that we are approaching the New World there is a lookout placed in the crow's nest at all times to sight land. "How I wish I could be up there," I said to myself. Just then Mrs. Hopkins came by. I told her I would be fourteen on the day after tomorrow. She smiled. "And for your birthday you shall have a fine gift," she promised. What could it be? I wonder.

November 9

I awoke this morning to the sound of the leadsman from
his perch outside the mizzen shrouds. He was chanting
the depth of the lead line. "Thirty, forty, fifty, sixty fathoms." It was not anything I hadn't heard before. Then he
yelled, "Eighty fathoms at the bottom, sir!"

I knew what it meant, Tom. I jumped out of the shallop
and made my way to the main deck. Others were already
coming alive, stumbling beside me. They'd heard, too. *Only
eighty fathoms at the bottom.* We were nearing land.

The deck was already crowded when I got there. A slight
morning breeze flapped the sails above us. In one direction
you could see the fading quarter moon, in another a light on
the horizon that would soon be the sun. Then a sound I
thought I'd never hear again. A gull, circling about over-
head. People all around me, with damp blankets wrapped
around them so they looked more like ghosts than humans,
pointed to the gull. Some fell right to their knees and called
on the Almighty. In that half-light it was right eerie, Tom, I
can tell you. We peered ahead to some distant mists that
clung to the water's surface. Then in the next moment
came the cry from the lookout far above. "Land ho!"

Women started crying. Men took off their hats and fell
to their knees. The younger men, like me, ran to the railing, asking, "Where, where?"

"There," an old seaman pointed.

"It's only the mist," John Howland said.

"If that's mist, lad, mayhap ye need another dip in the ocean to bring ye awake," said the old seaman. "It's land, I say. It's what we've come for. It's America."

I stared at it hard, Tom. A long, low line, grey and brown and not much to look at. I felt disappointment. Then the light in the east broke through some clouds and shone down, making clear the outline. I could see trees, a forest, sandy beaches. At that moment a whole flock of gulls swooped around our ship. I looked up. The breeze had picked up. The sails were filled and billowing. The water below had changed color, too. It was blue now instead of greenish black.

I felt a hand on my shoulder. "Didn't I say you'd have a fine birthday gift, Jasper?" I didn't have to look up, Tom. I knew it was Mrs. Hopkins. And when I did look up I saw she had her newborn son in her arms. She held him up high in his blanket. "There, Oceanus," she said, "there is your new home. There is America."

November 10

Tom, I do salute you from this new land, though I have not set foot upon it yet. None have. And here it is one day from when it was first sighted. We wait on the ship.

Arguments abound. The young men are restless and cannot abide a moment more aboard her. The women beg to be allowed to go ashore and wash the clothing that smells like some back alley in the poorest part of London. But what has bestirred the elders at long last is the lack of wood. Our supply is gone and there sit all those trees in the forest.

But everyone is muttering and arguing whether we should even step ashore here. Some hold that this is not the Hudson River. My master said God's winds have guided us here, in this place. Captain Jones said we could venture no closer for the shoals and rocks. Then John Howland, speaking for the older bond servants, said if this be not Virginia Company land, then when they go ashore the bound men will use their own liberty and no man should have the power to command them. The elders have no patent for this place. The bound servants stood firm, eleven of them, before Elders Bradford and Brewster. Then, before my master's eyes, Edward Dotey grabbed me and pulled me with them.

The leaders were alarmed. Especially Mr. Hopkins. "Is this by way of thanks for making you part of my family?" he asked. Dotey smiled. "We follow in kind what you did when you were shipwrecked in Bermuda," he said. For this Mr. Hopkins had no reply, and the mutineers stood firm. The leaders knew, of course, that they could not clear fields, hew timbers, or build houses without the help of these servants. So they retired to the captain's cabin for a day and a night to draw up a document.

They call it a covenant and say the laws they make will be for the good of all. They asked all to sign, even the troublemakers. I was too young. And no women signed. I heard Dotey say they are only chattel to be commanded by their men. Then, having pronounced us a "civil body politick," they elected John Carver as governor and tomorrow, at first light, we go ashore.

November 11

I am so weary, yet I must write. I have been ashore! Not all have, but I walked the New World. Such a scramble there was. Sixteen men went and I was allowed to accompany them, the reason being that my master came upon me last evening as I was writing and asked what I was about. I told him. He said that Elder Bradford spoke of keeping a book, but I should go with the first expedition on the morrow and record what I saw.

First we took the longboat, but could not reach land for the sandbars, so had to wade through three feet of freezing water. But once our feet touched land, I was no longer cold. We walked a while along the beach, carefully at first because the elders were looking for the tracks of cloven feet to see if the Evil One was here. We found none. Many of the men wore their steel breastplates and full armor. How strange it was to cast an eye to the nearby forest and not know what manner of beast was watching and might lunge out at us. But none did. After we went about two leagues, the men decided to venture into the woods onto a small neck of land. There we found holly trees, birch, ash, walnut, oaks, and sassafras. Trees, Tom! Such trees as they would kill for in London. Wood, timber, for burning, for warming, for building. Here in this place there are endless trees. We wonder, how far do they go on? I think forever, Tom. I think everything in this place goes on forever. I think that we have found Forever.

There was not much underbrush, thank heaven, but we soon discovered that on one side of this land was the bay and on the other the ocean. But no fresh water. We worked hard that afternoon cutting juniper trees and tying the wood into bundles and lugging it back to the ship. When we got back, everyone was waiting to hear what we found. When we told them how rich and black the earth was, they said more prayers of thanks. Fires were lighted, and for the first time in weeks we were able to eat hot food.

Tomorrow is the Sabbath, so the Saints announced they would not go ashore. More mutterings, now from Captain Jones's men. They grumble that soon the snow will fly. They threaten that if we don't move our puke-stockinged feet, they will toss us and our furnishings overboard so they can set sail for England. They forget we are not all puke-stockings.

After our last meal of the day I saw Mistress Bradford standing alone by the rail, gazing out at the land. "What is it like, Jasper?" she asked me. I told her how plentiful were the trees, how rich the soil, how I saw clams and mussels on the sandflats when the tide ran out. "It's a good place," I told her. "It is an endless maze," she said, "and there are no friends to welcome us, nor inns to entertain us and refresh our weather-beaten bodies. The whole place has a wild and savage hue."

I think that is how Forever would look, Tom, if you feared it. I think, too, that Mistress Bradford would not like it here in this place even if there were friends to welcome us. I think she did not wish to come.

November 13

Another day ashore! And while I write this, I have fearsome worry and fearsome joy. My worry is that I have no more shallop to sleep in, for it was taken ashore to be rebuilt and the carpenter says that might take weeks. I found an old piece of canvas and fashioned it into a hammock such as the sailors sleep in. It hangs in a quiet corner of the 'tween deck. Here I write. I miss the shallop, but my joy is that I wear clean clothing for the first time in weeks. My underclothes, shirt, and hosiery smell of the salt sea and the breath of air here in this place, which is sharp and free of the foul smells of London. All the women went ashore this day to wash the clothing. How they scrubbed! As if to wash the very stench of the Old World from our things.

It was a day of sun and bright sky. The small children went ashore. They dug clams and mussels, and, with the dogs, chased flocks of gulls. I explored with the expedition. The first thing we saw was a school of whales! They played hard near us, right off the shore, very near the *Mayflower*. One of the seamen fired his musket, but the gun only blew up in his face. I am glad, for the whales seem so playful. The Elders on the expedition decried the fact they hadn't brought tools to harvest oil from the whales. If they had, they could have paid back our debt to our London backers in two weeks, instead of the months that farming and fishing will take.

A league or so down the beach we espied some men with a dog. Miles Standish, who led us, urged caution for surely they were savages. Savages with a dog! Where did they get a dog? He played about on the beach just like our dogs. We were prepared to meet the savages, our first in the New World, but as soon as they espied us they disappeared into the woods. The dog did not. He kept running toward us. Captain Standish said whatsoever we did, we must not shoot the dog or we would have war before we officially claimed this place. He ordered us to double time, and give chase to the men in the woods. As we did so, a sharp whistle came from the forest and the dog, too, disappeared. But we followed, seeking their footings. One man said we were being foolish: the Indians might be planning to ambush and kill us all. I must confess, Tom, I was fearful. But I would not let anyone know of it. At any rate, soon we were in such darkness as we could scarce see. Our clothing was torn by brambles and thorns. We followed Captain Standish for what seemed like an hour before we came out of the woods onto the bay shore. There were some large clearings. And we could see they had once been cornfields. Here we made a fire and camped for the night.

Our hands and faces were cut by the undergrowth in the thickets. We had some biscuits and cheese, then they passed around a flask of brandy. Elder Bradford said I might have a sip as there was no water. I got out my book, quill pen, and ink and commenced to write, close enough to the fire that I could see. The men watched me, then Mr. Hopkins asked what I was writing. I told them that it was an account of my adventures for you. They then inquired how I had come to write, an indentured boy as I was. So I told them about our father and how we were not always poor. Elder Bradford nodded and said, "Give a good account of us, boy, do not revile the truth." I said I would.

November 14

This day we breakfasted on our poor victuals, prayed, and moved on. Soon we came upon a valley full of bayberry, long grasses, and brush. A number of little paths ran through it, and we soon discovered why. Water! The first fresh water we had found since we dropped anchor! It was a small pond and Elder Bradford bade us all stand in a circle. "We graciously believe the Lord is with us," he said. "As we drink this first water in a new land let us be nourished by it and prosper in our endeavors." And so we sat down and drank. Elder Bradford then said he had never tasted of the wine at the Court of King James, but he supposed this to be a headier brew.

After that we came upon some large clearings which must have been used by the Indians as cornfields. Here we found many carefully built mounds of sand. One was covered with grass mats and had a piece of arched wood over it. Soon we were on our hands and knees digging into it with shells.

I found some arrows. I had never touched an Indian

arrow, and I ran my hands over it. What fine work, Tom! I wanted to have it, to keep it, to bring it back to the ship and show everyone. Someday I would show it to you. I asked Captain Standish if I could keep it. "No," he said, "for this is likely a grave. See the bow they have put with the arrows? When Indians bury a warrior they send him on his way with all he needs." He then said we must respect their graves. So I put the arrow back.

We restored the grave and proceeded on. We came to a small river, which Captain Standish said could one day be used as a harbor. After that we climbed a sandy hill and found a large meadow on the other side. More heaps of sand, freshly made. Surely there could not be that many graves. So we decided to investigate.

In the first one we found a large basket that Captain Standish pronounced very handsomely and cunningly made. In it were four bushels of corn, some still in the ears. There was some discussion as to whether we should take it or not. "Certainly God has led us to it," Elder Bradford said. "It is a gift to us from the very ground here. From this new land. What think you, Captain Standish?" Captain Standish said he didn't have frequent discourse with God, but that we certainly needed the corn. And that we should post a guard at that very moment if we meant to take it. So we did.

"When we are established as a plantation we will grow

our own and return it in kind," said Elder Bradford. So we took it along. Some men stuffed ears of it in their pockets. It was yellow, red, and blue. Indeed there was too much to carry, so we left some.

Before we left, we looked around at the fine country and espied a small river to the south. We commenced marching, staying one behind the other. Soon we found two canoes, one on either side of the river, as people would do who would ferry back and forth.

We stood and looked at each other. The country was occupied, this we knew. For all we knew, the occupants could be watching us at that moment, ready to let fly an abundance of arrows. We must be careful. We wanted to investigate the river to find fresh water, but that would mean going miles inland. Governor Carver had said to remain out no more than two days.

So we made our way back to the freshwater pond, set good watch, and camped the night, making sure to burn a goodly fire so those aboard the ship could see we were still alive.

November 15

Last night I heard beasts in the forests, cries that bore no likeness to those of any man. Twice I woke at the sound. Were the beasts angry that we were here? I shivered. It was so cold! All around me were huddled forms. The fire burned brightly, however, and our guards were alert. At the second waking, I climbed out from under my blanket and made my way to one of them. It was Mr. Tilley. "What is that sound?" I asked. "We know not, lad," he answered. "It could be the Evil One for all we know. But we are at the ready. Have no fear. Whatever it is will not venture from the forest." I went back to my blanket and lay awake, gazing at the stars, and thought that we would all perish in this wilderness. Then I thought of Elder Bradford, a scholar, a man of goodly inheritance. He'd sold his house in Holland and given all he had to come here.

I thought of my master, always so severe. Yet he is made of both iron and velvet. His anger comes slowly, but his will is strong. He drinks only water when others drink beer. He, too, is from the upper classes, but threw his fortunes in with these people. His fortunes and his life. The printing shop where he worked in Holland was ransacked, which is why he woke me that night to flee with him to England. Since our time there, he has shown me many small kindnesses that other masters do not show their bound servants.

I thought of all the other good people I'd come to know on the ship. Edward Winslow, a man of property and education. Isaac Allerton, a tailor. Will Mullins, who made shoes. John Alden, a cooper. The women who had rocked and soothed the children, prayed through the storms at sea, and never complained.

What gave us the right to think we could cross the ocean and start a new world? But I knew. My master had told me.

Queen Elizabeth, who came before King James, had cut off the head of Mary Stuart, her cousin who was Queen of Scotland. She thought Mary was sending servants to poison her. Then Queen Elizabeth said to her people, "It was wrong to cut off this woman's head. I had no part in it. It is the fault of my Secretary of State, Mr. Davison." She sent Davison to the Tower of London. Davison's clerk was my master Elder Brewster, who knew the only thing he could do was leave court. After all, the Queen might take his head, too. You can never tell with queens.

So Elder Brewster went back to Scrooby Manor, his home. And prayed and plotted and waited and held secret Sabbath meetings. And he and his friends became a congregation. In 1603, King James came to the throne. Elder Brewster and his congregation in Scrooby went to Holland. They spent over ten years there. But their children began to take on the ways of Holland, ways too free for their parents' liking. They were afraid their children would forget they were English. So they looked for someplace else to live. But where? Guiana? Sir Walter Raleigh had gone there, and where was he now? In the Tower! The coast of South America? Too hot.

America, some said. They'd heard about this place, far across the ocean. True, expeditions there had failed. People in Maine and Roanoke were never heard from again. Jamestown was a financial failure. What about the area around the Hudson River? The Dutch were doing well there.

Cold, someone else said. Ice and snow, savages, and beasts.

Never mind. Elder Brewster and his congregation decided to take their chances with the savages and beasts. They know why they are here. And so do I.

November 17

In the morning we made our way through the forest and back to the *Mayflower* in freezing rain and wind. We were tramping through the woods when we espied a sapling bent low and forming an arch over our path. Stephen Hopkins warned us that he had seen such traps in Virginia. "Indians trap deer in them," he said. "Be careful."

But Elder Bradford, last in our single line of march, did not hear this. He stepped right into the trap and was soon dangling upside down by one leg. When we had loosed him finally, he said the trap was "a very pretty device, made with a rope of their own making and having a noose as cunningly designed as any roper in England can make."

We tried hunting, Tom. There were deer in abundance, also partridges, great scores of geese and ducks. But our matchlocks were too clumsy, the men too noisy, and we knew we would have to learn more about this place before we brought home such bounty. So we waded some tidal creeks, and lugged our corn over sand bars until we finally found the beach again. One man fired his musket and a party came to welcome us from the *Mayflower.*

They called our expedition Second Discovery. All were thankful for the corn. Elder Bradford told us that when Israelites entered the Promised Land they too had gone with sixteen men and brought back the fruit of the land for their brethren. Everyone was marvelously glad. Afterward, when we went our separate ways, Mistress Bradford came upon me. "They were not sixteen," she said, "they were twelve. You made them twelve." I nodded. "Why did you not say?" she asked. "Because," I answered, "I would not disabuse them of their feeling that this is their Promised Land." It is no promised land, she told me. "It is a wild and desperate place." Then she disappeared into the bowels of the ship.

I saw a light in her eyes, Tom, that came from no warmth inside. It was most strange, and it frightened me. For a moment I pondered going to her husband and asking him to comfort her. But then, what right had I do this, a mere bound boy? I did not go. I spent hours afterward thinking. Should I have?

November 20

Of a sudden things have come to a halt. We wait for the shallop to be repaired so we can explore farther and find a place to settle. The weather has turned even colder and we have no shelter on land. Everyone argues the matter. Some want to settle here and start building now. Others say no, we must find a better harbor that can welcome ships for trade. That this place has only small freshwater ponds that may dry up in the summer. No matter where I go on this ship there are people huddled in heated discourse. Some will not talk to others. How can people stand up to a king and be so brave on the one hand and so mean on the other? Elder Bradford said that someday generations to come will honor us for what we do here.

How? We are dirty and hungry. We smell. We fight with each other. We grumble and are sore afraid. How?

I try to get ashore each day to get away from the ship, if only to bring back wood. The food aboard is fast dwindling and of poor quality. The crew grumbles that the victuals will not last the winter. They say we should settle somewhere or surely they will put us off the boat.

November 21

Today I minded Damaris. I read to her from a book my master gave me. Also I was given some of the corn to shell for seed for spring. It was put in the common store.

November 22

This day I did not go ashore, though I'd planned to. I came upon Mrs. Bradford, crying. "Can I do anything for you, Mistress?" I asked. "Shall I fetch your husband?" She said her husband was too busy being an important Elder to care about her tears. "Today he might walk the waves, I cannot disturb him," she said. Tom, I think there is a hint of madness in this woman, but I told her only to hush, that I would read to her if she wished. She bade me sit at the foot of her bunk and do so. While I was so engaged, Edward Dotey and Edward Leister came by, grunted, kicked my leg, and sneered. Then turned and gave me a look such as would wither the cockles of anyone's heart. I shall suffer a bit for my kindness to Mrs. Bradford, but I care not.

November 23

I almost had a fight today. I was getting ready to leave the ship to go ashore when Edward Dotey and Edward

Leister came upon me. "Where are you off to, little wharf rat?" Dotey asked. I told him I was going to find wood. He laughed and asked, "Wouldn't you rather sit on the bunk of Mistress Bradford?" I told him not to revile the name of such a good woman. "You rotten little maggot," he said, "always looking for favor. No wonder you get to go on expeditions while we fester on this old tub." I told them kindness was not looking for favor. "Then why didn't you stand firm with us when we argued about our liberty before going ashore?" Leister asked. I told them I was too young to have a voice in such matters. They began pushing me about while accusing me of other things. They said I was becoming a puke-stocking and gave me a hard push. I fell and my book tumbled out of my pocket. They grabbed it up and began to ruffle through it. I demanded it back, one word led to another, and there is no telling what would have happened had not Mr. Hopkins come along. "Are you coming ashore, lad?" he asked me. I said yes, as soon as I reclaimed my property. He only had to look at Dotey for him to give my book back to me. As I was climbing down the rope ladder to the longboat, Dotey peered over at me. "You're still a puke-stocking," he said. "It's only because you write drivel that they let you go along. Not because you're of value as a man. Why don't you stay aboard and hold the hands of the women?"

Dotey and Leister are big and strong. Why won't Mr.

Hopkins take them? True, they are feisty and bold, but so is he. Should I ask Mr. Hopkins to take them next time? Why should I? I'm not a puke-stocking. Or any of the other things they call me.

November 27

The shallop is finally pronounced ready to sail. Another expedition is planned. Talk and speculation run wild. Who will go? Where will they go? How soon? Today I approached my master and told him Dotey and Leister wished to be included. He nodded but said only that he would bring the matter up for discussion.

December 4

Edward Thompson, a young servant of Will White, died yesterday, coughing and worn thin. It bodes no good. Many others are coughing and taken ill, too. The elders say we can delay no longer. If there is to be another expedition, let us proceed. But where to? They have consulted second mate Robert Coppin. He has been to these shores before. He pointed across the bay, saying there lies a good harbor, less than twenty-four leagues away. I am selected to go with many others. We go on the morrow. Dotey is to go, but not Leister. After Leister was told, I saw him huddled with Francis Billington, who is my age and a troublemaker. The whole family bodes trouble. Always arguing, raising doubts, causing rifts among the passengers. I think no good will come of those two putting their heads together.

December 5

I was right, and sorry I did not bring the matter of Leister and Billington to someone's attention. But I could prove no wrong intent. Yet, this day as we readied to leave on the expedition we were halted by a great explosion. It came from 'tween decks. Here had been put, for safety, the men's weapons. Also a small barrel of black powder. The explosion, caused when young Billington primed a musket near the gunpowder, provoked panic. Portholes blew out, the deck shook, people screamed, and all went running. No one was hurt, so of course the Saints said it was God's own divine providence.

Captain Jones had a different opinion. I thought he would kill or maim young Billington. He grabbed him and shook him, banishing him to the hold for the day. Such swearing I never heard from any man. "This is my ship!" he yelled. "She is a sweet ship. She never carried passengers before. Only cognac, English cloth, taffetas, satins, wine. Never before has she suffered the stink of people. Now she brings you across demon seas to a new land. And you would blow her up? Never again, never, will I have people as cargo!"

In my presence Mr. Hopkins asked Leister if he had a hand in the mischief. Leister said no. I said nothing. Apologies were made to the captain by the elders. All needed comfort. So our expedition was called off. I saw Leister grinning at my disappointment.

Did he put Billington up to this? To what end? What befalls one of us befalls us all. What benefits one serves all. We go ashore for the common good. Governor Carver is bringing his servant, John Howland. Mr. Hopkins has decided to bring Leister, too. I think he is fearful of leaving him on board.

December 6

Finally we departed in early afternoon, delayed because the weather was sore unfit. Winds raged, snow fell with biting coldness on our faces.

Second Mate Coppin was at the tiller. We made for what he called Thievish Harbor, so named because one of the savages stole a harpoon from his party when they visited it last year.

There are eighteen of us, myself included. Many are sick unto death. Mr. Tilley and the master gunner swooned with the cold. Ice formed on the breastplates of Captain Standish and others. As for the rest of us, the wind whipped water on us and it froze on our clothing. I shivered more than on that rainy night we were caught on London's streets with no place to sleep. Remember, Tom?

How awful it was! We sailed on for about twenty leagues, then made for shore where we sighted about a dozen savages surrounding a large black thing on the beach. We landed, and Elder Bradford picked me up so I wouldn't have to wade through the freezing water. I wished he hadn't, for Dotey and Leister sneered at me all the while.

The savages ran into the woods when they saw us. Dotey, Leister, and I were told to make a fire. All the time we chopped and hauled wood, they mocked me. "Don't think because you didn't tell on me that you are in our favor," Leister said. I told them I didn't want to be in their favor, thank you. Then Elder Bradford said we should build a barricado of logs to keep out the cold. This being done, we huddled 'round the fire and made camp, for it was, by now, dusk.

December 7

In the morning we divided, some in the shallop and some along the shore. I was with the group to stay on land. So was Dotey. We found the great black thing the Indians had been working on. It was, said Captain Standish, a grampus. Tom, it was about fifteen feet long! Never have I seen such. Its back was black, its underbelly white. Elder Bradford said it contained valuable oils which we could use, had we the time and tools to harvest it.

We went on, following Indian tracks. Very soon we came to a large piece of ground with sand mounds, and fences around it. Fences! These savages fenced in their graveyards! "We will dig nothing here," Elder Bradford announced. He was given no argument. Were these victims of the plague? An air of despair hung over everything. Such silence! So many graves! Would we come to the same end in this place? I know the question gnawed at all. Again we went on, this time coming to some deserted wigwams. We stayed here the afternoon, searching, but found nothing. A town without people. How eerie. We then walked miles along the beach to meet up with the shallop. There we had to chop more wood for a barricado for the night. Nothing to eat but biscuits and salt meat. Dotey and Leister grumbled. Mr. Hopkins told them to hold still the tongues in their head or next time they would stay in the ship's hold. I was one of the last to sleep, and was sitting by the fire writing when the sentry cried, "To arms, to arms!"

I jumped up and near spilled my ink. The men were

lining the walls of the barricado with the muskets at the ready. I wished I had one. I know I could learn to shoot.

"'Tis but the howling of wolves," said a seaman from the shallop. So all finally went to sleep, myself included, though it seemed but a blink of time before they were waking me.

December 8

We woke in the dark. They were making breakfast of such victuals as we had. Then some started carrying their muskets and armor to the shallop. Captain Standish advised against this. "Do not leave yourself unprotected," he said. But they continued doing so.

We were sitting to plan our day when we heard a horrible cry from the woods. "Woach! Woach! Ha! Ha! Woach!" It came from all sides. It echoed. We were surrounded by it. Captain Standish immediately fired his gun, as did another man. How the sound echoed across the water! The other men dashed for the shallop to get their guns, but before we knew it, an Indian stood behind a tree, then others ran onto the beach, sealing them off. Savages, Tom! With paint on their faces. Tall and fearless, with scarce any clothing against the biting cold. Earrings they wore, and their long hanging necklaces made of shells. There on the beach they planted their feet firm in the sand

and stood their ground. Never have I seen such beautiful warriors, though I once saw the King's soldiers in London.

There was an air about them of simple cleanness, of straight truth. Does that sound silly? If you saw them you would say no. Here is something new, I thought, yet something as old as time. Very soon, however, Captain Standish fired at them. I wanted to yell, "No, no, don't kill them. We need them!" God be praised, the captain missed. The savages fled, quick as deer. They all fled, quick as they'd come. We stood alone on the beach in the whipping wind, wondering if we'd dreamed them.

Mayhap we are dreaming now. Mayhap we will wake up of a sudden and find ourselves back on the streets of Holland.

We looked to the forest then, and by the fickle light of morning saw them there in the woods, running back and forth. All were for leaving then, but Captain Standish said, "No, no, we must show them we are not to be dallied with. Who will come with me into the woods?"

Several men went while the rest of us waited. Had I a gun I would have gone. We heard them there in the forest, shouting, then shooting off their muskets. While this was going on, Elder Bradford bade me help him pick their arrows from the wood of our barricado. Altogether we found eighteen. Some had arrowheads of brass, some of horn, others were made of the claws of eagles. Elder

Bradford said yes, I might keep one. I can't wait to show it to you, Tom.

We knew how blessed we were. So we set off in the shallop much thankful. As soon as we pushed off, the weather turned foul again, and by mid-afternoon we had a regular gale. The rudder of the shallop broke and two of the men did all they could do to steer her. "Press on," Coppin yelled, "I see the harbor!"

The flood tide swept us along. I hung on for dear life. The mast broke in three places. The wind was so wild we could not speak to one another. Coppin gestured, pointing as the shallop rode the waves into a cove. "I have seen this place before," Coppin yelled.

"God guide us to a safe place!" Elder Bradford prayed.

We went ashore. But where were we? Were there savages waiting to kill us? Some wanted to stay the night in the shallop, but First Mate Clark jumped out. "I don't care if I'm killed," he said, "I must needs make a fire." Others followed and soon had a fire started. It was so dark we did not know where we were or if we would be killed that night by savages.

December 9

With the morning light, Mate Coppin looked around him and said yes, this is the harbor he recalled. We were on an island. And the men named it Clark's Island for the chief mate who was brave enough to be first to step ashore last night. I wished we could explore, but Elder Bradford said that God had given us a sweet day and we would rest and clean the muskets and give God thanks for His mercies. Some said that the Sabbath was the morrow. "There are enough mercies for two days' rest and thanks," Bradford said. So we didn't get to explore until Monday.

December 11

A sad and a happy day. The sun shone down on our beautiful place. The sun shone down on our beautiful place. The sailors put a new mast on the shallop and we sailed across the harbor. The water sparkled, the sun had warmth. Going ashore we found running brooks, good earth, trees aplenty and, with the good harbor, this was declared the place where we would build our homes.

All were so eager to impart the news that it was decided to sail right across the harbor instead of hugging the shoreline. Twenty-five miles in open water. But the wind was kind and the sun warm, and so by late afternoon we were back to the *Mayflower*. As we scrambled aboard, the married men could scarce wait to see their families and tell the news.

On deck they awaited us, a quiet group, though wives came forward to greet their husbands. "We have found our home," Elder Bradford announced. "We have decided to call the harbor Plymouth, as from the place where we started our journey."

All wanted to hear of the place, and we told, each of us, what we had seen. Of course, Edward Dotey made it sound as if he had frightened off the Indians all on his own. Then, of a sudden, in the midst of all the talk Elder Bradford looked around. "Where is my wife?" he asked. "Where is Dorothy?"

The talk stopped. Everyone just stood and stared. All we could hear for the moment was the cry of a gull swooping over the ship. Then Captain Jones stepped forward. "Good man," he said. "It pleased God to take your wife this day. She fell into the water and drowned."

Elder Bradford wept. People gathered round him. "What happened?" he asked. "How could this befall her? Why was I not here to save her? How did she fall? How?"

No one answered. Nothing was said. I looked around me at the faces on the deck, but no one would meet my eyes. All looked away, or cast their eyes down. It was then that I knew what they all knew, Tom. What they would not speak if a savage stood over them with his hatchet at the ready.

What happened this day did not please God at all. Dorothy Bradford had jumped from the ship into the water. She had taken her own life.

Afterward, when all dispersed, I heard Dotey say to Leister, "I told you she was daft." He said it loud enough so I could hear. Later that night my master came and stood before me as I lay in my hammock in the Great Cabin, writing. "Jasper," he said. I started to get to my feet, as is my custom when speaking to my master, but he motioned me to be still. "You write in this book of yours everything that befalls us," he said. I nodded yes. "I ask you not to write any thought you may have on the death of Mistress Bradford, excepting to say she fell from the ship. Do you understand, Jasper?"

"But, Master," I said. He nodded. "Yes, Jasper?" I told him I would fain put a question to him. He nodded again. "Have we crossed the demon seas," I asked, "at the risk of life and limb, eaten food with maggots in it, worn befouled clothing, and walked on earth never before walked on by Englishmen, to be told that we cannot think or write what we believe?"

He sighed and shook his head and looked at his hat in his hands. "She was so young," he said. "Only eighteen." Then he looked at me. "Why did I have to have a boy put to me who has the mind of a scholar?" he asked. And then he walked away.

December 20

After much argument and discussion, I think the elders have finally found a place to make our home. These people do make much discussion of every matter. Some like this land above what they now call Plymouth Harbor, but other feel it is too heavily wooded to be cleared for houses.

I have been allowed to go ashore with those who must learn more. We have found fat soil, goodly groves of trees, fowls in abundance, berries, sorrel, liverwort, yarrow, watercress, leeks, and onions. Tom, if the people in London had what is here, no one would be poor. The ship's carpenter came and said that the gravel and clay were good for building. And there was much fine stone.

When it came time to make a decision no one could agree. Elder Bradford said we would call on God for direction. After all, we have but meager food left and all the beer is gone, except that for the captain and the crew.

Whatever God said to Elder Bradford, no one knows, but a decision has been reached. We shall make our home above the harbor. Much of the ground was grown before in corn, by Indians. There is a hill on which they can make a fort. Captain Standish wishes to place a cannon there as soon as we can. There are sweet streams for water and fish. The harbor will welcome shallops and small boats. A large rock sits there which cannot be moved, but mayhap we can find a use for it.

December 21

Mary Allerton, wife of the tailor, was brought to bed of a child. But it was dead born. Richard Britteridge also died. We have started our cemetery before we start our homes. It is on a low hill they have named Burial Hill, just above that big rock.

December 24

Tomorrow is Christmas. Tom, do you recollect Christmas when Mother was yet alive and we had our home above the clock shop when we were but children? Was that us? Or did I dream it? Here the Saints and Strangers argue again, this time about Christmas. The Strangers and crew wish to celebrate Christmas. The Saints say that such an observance, either by forbearing labor, feasting, or any other way, is abhorrent to them. That is part of the Roman corruption, that no one knows when Christ was born and Christ would not want his birthday celebrated in such a pagan way. I reverence my master but wonder how he knows what Christ would wish. We all celebrate our birthdays.

December 25

Cold and gale force winds. All able-bodied men went ashore to fell timber. The Common House is to be built on the north bank of the brook, above the beach. The sand was dug, the foundation started this day. I am worn to the bone. Dotey and Leister were set to gathering branches and wood to make cone-shaped shelters for any who stay ashore. My master set me to working with them. They are strong and vigorous. We worked together, but they did not speak except to order me about. I was determined to show them I could pull my weight.

On board in the evening, the captain was intent on celebrating Christmas. He is Church of England. He has broken open a barrel of the ship's beer and invited all to partake there. The Saints declined. I did not. I am no Saint nor have I the desire to be.

December 28

For two days there was no going ashore to work. A fearful wind and storm came upon us. Snow and sleet and rain.

But today we did get back to work. The elders took measurements for the main street in our village. It is to go up the hill to the fort. They speak of building nineteen houses. Unmarried men will be put with families. The ship is a mile and half from shore and everything we bring from it must be dragged up the hill. Many grumble.

January 1, 1621

Degory Priest died this day. He was a hatter. Tom, betimes in the middle of my work I look around me into the woods that stretch on, so bleak, into nothing, and at the emptiness of the shore, where the water is churning up waves and I cannot but think, what are we about here? Today at Degory Priest's burial I thought, whyfore do we need a hatter? Will this land ever support us so that people can have shops? I think not, Tom.

January 2

We work on the Common House. It is to be of wattle and daub construction with a thatched roof. All work on it, even the women, who carry things or help their husbands by handing them tools. Others watch children so mothers can work. They have a plan for the first house. I have seen it. It will be a wood frame house with a stone foundation.

We carry stones that we hunt in the woods and fields. I am helping to mix the clay that seals the seams.

January 3

All the while we work, we see the smoke from distant fires. And we know the savages are watching us. Will they burn what we build?

January 4

Captain Standish took some men and went to find the savages. Mayhap, he said, we could meet with them. But they could not be found. Standish and his men returned with an eagle they had shot and the women cooked it over the fire. It had a wonderful taste. I could not believe I was eating something that was not fish or salted meat. Captain Jones said we should fish for our supper, but we are sick to death of fish.

January 6

Our Common House is near finished. It only wants thatching. It is twenty feet square. We will use it for shelter until the houses are built. I walked through it when all left, Tom, and thought I was in the Church of

St. Peter in Leyden. Remember the house my master had in Leyden in the Stinksteeg? And Groenehuis, owned by Mr. Brewer, the printer? I think our Common House is better.

A house, Tom! The first I will sleep in since we were put out of ours in London! And no one can put me out. I have earned my right to it! I saw it in the making. I helped make it. I wish you were here to have use of it with me. Now they speak of houses for everyone. They have decided that each family will build its own. "By that course men will make more haste," my master said.

January 7

The Common House is not without cost. Christopher Martin is taken ill from working in the cold and from the scarcity of food these past weeks. So is Elder Bradford. He was working one minute on his own house and collapsed the next with headache and fever. We expect him to die. All are praying.

January 9

Francis Billington, the younger of the troublemaker brothers, announced at the evening meal that he has discovered a sea from atop a great tree. He plagued us about it so, one of the ship's mates went off with him to find it. They came back and announced it was a freshwater lake with many fish. Billington is preening like a peacock about this discovery. I wish I could do something like that to make everyone take notice of me. I want so to do something important to prove myself.

January 12

We are greatly troubled. Peter Browne and John Goodman went off with Goodman's dogs to gather thatch, and never came back. As dark came upon us, we went to the edge of the woods with lighted torches, calling their names. Only flickering shadows answered. We fear them dead by the hand of savages. We went back to the ship as snow came. If the savages don't get them, the cold surely will. I wanted to stay with those who are caring for Elder Bradford, but my master said no.

January 13

All worked in silence this day as we mourned the absence of Browne and Goodman. Dotey says they could never be taken with those dogs, especially the mastiff. She is most fierce. I prayed in my heart all day that he was right. Benumbed with cold, we were gathered to return to the ship for supper when we heard the yelping of what could only be Goodman's spaniel. I ran with the other young men into the darkness to see Browne and Goodman limping toward us from the wood, the dogs running ahead of them. A great cheer went up from us, and the others came to greet them.

Here is what happened, Tom. The dogs raised a buck in the woods and the men wanted to shoot it. They went racing after the dogs and soon became lost. They wandered all afternoon. When the snow came, they near froze. They fell asleep at night next to a tree, with the dogs as warmth, and were wakened by what they thought were lions coming at them. Goodman had all he could do to hold onto the mastiff, who wanted to engage the beasts in a fight. As it turned out, they were wolves. Goodman says the wolves sat and grinned at them for most of the night, but did not attack for the men throwing sticks and the dogs growling. The next day they found their way back to us, for which we are grateful.

January 14

This night, as we gathered for supper on the ship, we heard a cry from those on shore: "Fire! Fire!" Sure enough, we saw flames licking at the thatch on the roof of the Common House. Had the Indians attacked? We scrambled over the side into the shallop. When we got to shore, we found our friends fighting the fire. Someone had lighted a fire in the fireplace to see how the chimney would draw. A spark flew upwards into the roof thatch. But no great damage was done. None of the beams caught, though we feared for Elder Bradford, who still lies sick within.

January 15

I visited Elder Bradford in the Common House today. "Is there anything I can get you?" I asked him. "Oh, Jasper," he said, "I crave some beer." Without asking, I got into the shallop the next time they took it to the ship and sought out the bo'sun to ask him for some beer for Elder Bradford. He was most crude and cruel. "Beer for a puke-stocking?" he asked. "If it were my own father he should have none." I then took matters into my own hands and sought out Captain Jones in his cabin. He never sides with his men against the passengers, and I chanced incurring his anger for carrying tales. I told him what was said by his bo'sun and he was most sympathetic. "Beer for them that have need of it," he told his men. "Though we drink water homeward bound." And I was given a jug to take back to shore.

Of course when Dotey and Leister heard of it they

sought me out. "Still buttering up, hey, wharf rat?" they asked me. I care not if they think this is buttering up, Tom. Elder Bradford is a good man and you don't have to be a Saint to know it. I wish there had been someone in prison to grant our father's wishes when he was in dire need.

January 16

I forgot to write this yesterday. Many on board the *Mayflower* are sickly. Three of the mates, the master gunner, and the cook complain of pains, fever, and the chills as come with the ague.

January 20

Captain Jones today espied two Indians watching the ship from Clark's Island. They watch us all the time but do not show themselves. We worry they will attack those who stay ashore some night. Or even in God's good sunlight. I wonder, what would I do if they did? I asked my master if I could learn to use a musket, that I was near as tall as he and of a good strong build. He took my measure with his eyes and said he would pray on the matter and let me know.

January 25

We have greater worries. More are down sick in the Common House. There seems to be a general sickness that attacks all, more fearful than tomahawk or Indian torch. Governor Carver lies next to Elder Bradford. Captain Standish's wife Rose is taken and Mary Allerton whose babe was dead born. William White who hails from Sturton le Steeple, William Mullins, his wife and Stephen Hopkins. I worry for Mrs. Hopkins, with a new baby, but she seems confident he will recover. The ship's physician surgeon, Giles Heale, and Doctor Fuller physick them until they cry for mercy. I shall not get sick, Tom, I vow it. Do you recollect what father said when he called the doctor for mother when she had the smallpox? Doctors only kill you. I shall not let them put their hands on me.

February 2

All who do not work on the houses tend the sick. Dotey and Leister came up to me today. "You be a fool if you work with the sick, wharf rat," Dotey said to me. "They are puking and befouled. You will soon lie with them. We shall not. We work on the houses."

I stood looking after them as they walked off. Were

they right? Just then Mrs. Hopkins happened by with little Oceanus in her arms and Giles, Constance, and Damaris trailing after her. "Jasper, pay them no mind," she said. "My husband is down sick and so they make bolder than ever. You will not lie amongst the sick, though you work to help them. The abundance of toil and hazard of health will not harm you. Your master helps. So does Captain Standish. The Lord will uphold you, Jasper. You will grow and prosper in this land and so will your children."

"Are you faring well, mistress?" I asked her. She said yes. "They do not help you with the children as they should," I complained. She smiled and said that they were working on her house, which would be the first ready for habitation because her husband would be well soon. She had a firmness of voice as she'd had when she told me I would get a wonderful birthday present, just before land was sighted. So I believed her. And I took myself to the Common House to help. There they gave me the job of fetching wood and keeping the fire going. Dotey and Leister stayed outside, working on the houses.

February 8

Captain Standish's wife Rose died this day. We have taken to burying our dead by night so the Indians do not know how our ranks are thinning. We make no grave-stones or markers lest they see them. We trample the earth flat over them, as if they had never been.

February 10

It has pleased God to take to Him both the Tilleys and their wives and the mother, father, and brother of Priscilla Mullins. She is but eighteen. I speak now my master's words. I do not know how taking the parents of Priscilla could please God. I saw her crying this day. He also took William White and his two servants, leaving the wife with two very small children, one a suckling babe. We hear matters are even worse on board the *Mayflower*, that she has lost half her ship's company. Though many still sleep on her, I have asked permission to sleep in a corner of the Common House, wrapped in blankets. Yes, the sick lie here, but so do they lie on the ship. And the Common House is cleaner.

At night I wake to see the large shadows of those who tend the sick. I hear cries of anguish, prayers, moans. But I would rather be here than on the ship where the sailors rave and curse not only at us, but at their families.

One of the Saints went this day to tend the very bo'-sun who would not give Elder Bradford the beer. He died in delirium, praying. "Oh," he said to the woman who cared for him, "you, I now see, show your love like Christians indeed one to another, but we let one another lie and die like dogs." I do not mourn the villain's passing.

February 13

It has pleased God to make well Stephen Hopkins and Elder Bradford. It has pleased me that Mrs. Hopkins was right about her husband.

February 17

One of our number was out hunting waterfowl, hiding in the reeds on the bank of a stream. He saw a dozen of the savages. They were all painted! He ran to give the alarm to us. This evening Captain Standish, fresh from his grief over his wife, called a meeting in the Common House for the establishment of military order. All the young men, even the servants, stood at the ready to serve him. As Dotey and Leister rushed into line, I looked across the room at my master. I have come to read and understand his expressions. And he mine. He nodded yes, that I could join the line ready to serve, without my asking. So I took my place in line, too. No one ordered me away. No one would dare. My master has much eminence.

February 20

This day we sighted two Indians across the brook on what we call Strawberry Hill. They made signs to us, bidding us to come. Captain Standish would not let us go to them. He bade us stay back, but went himself with Stephen Hopkins. They took but one musket between them. We held our breaths as they walked across the brook and laid down the musket as a sign of peace. "They will be slaughtered now," Dotey said. How I wish he would shut his foul mouth. The Indians would not abide their coming, but ran off.

February 21

We younger men served Standish this day. Under his direction we helped Captain Jones and what is left of his crew bring ashore a small cannon. It weighed some 1,200 pounds. How we struggled! On the beach we already had a larger cannon with a range of 360 yards. It took us all afternoon to drag these up the hill and mount them on a wooden platform. Now our artillery is in place.

February 22

Captain Standish went with four men to investigate the whereabouts of the savages whose fires we see burning in the distance. They found no savages, but came back with an eagle that they shot on the way home. We have been so longing for fresh meat that we cooked and ate it that night. It was very good.

March 1

I have not written, Tom, because death has come and come again amongst us. Before February was finished died Mrs. Isaac Allerton; Elizabeth, the wife of Edward Winslow; and betimes two or three of a day. All this while there were but less than a dozen to attend them. All work on the houses has come to a stop. Dotey and Leister are set to digging graves.

Disease has taken whole families. Only three wedded couples have not had their union broken by death. Half the households have lost their heads. Thomas Tinker, his wife, and his son are dead. John Turner and his two sons. Richard Gardiner. Christopher Martin and his wife. John Rigdale and his wife. Oh, there are too many to name. But Elder Bradford lives. So do my master, his wife, and sons. Mrs. Hopkins lives, as do her husband and two children.

John Alden lives. So do Dotey and Leister, the whole Billington family, and John Howland, who fell overboard on the ship. Isaac Allerton has lost his wife. There are now many orphans to be taken in by other families. I do not feel so alone anymore.

We tend the sick all day. We fetch firewood, heat water for washing, clean them, cook for them, feed them, pray for them. My master is tireless though he is over fifty years of age. Once he saw me in the Common House. "You still here, Jasper?" he asked. "Why don't you take yourself outside for a while? Go play with my sons." I think he worries for me.

And so I went out into the bright March sunlight, surprised to see that the sky is still blue and the gulls still circling above, when so many have died. Love, who is nine, and Wrestling, who is six, pestered me to play throw ball with them. I did so, though I took no joy in the game. Betimes I feel a hundred years old, Tom, instead of fourteen.

March 2

This day all worked again caring for the sick. At supper, aboard the ship, I brought my master a plate of food because he just sat there and seemed too tired to come to the table. "Come, eat with me, Jasper," he said. So I fetched my own plate and sat with him.

"My eldest son, Jonathan, did not wish to come to America," he told me. "He wished to stay in Holland and look after the girls." I said nothing, for I did not know in which direction his conversation was going. "The girls could have stayed with friends," he went on. "I think Jonathan feared this place, Jasper."

I said naught. Then he spoke again. "His fear is just." Again I said nothing. In a short while he smiled at me. "I'm glad you've come," he said. And I felt warm and loved. Tom, I think he not only bears affection for me, I think he compares me with Jonathan and finds Jonathan wanting. I must work hard to deserve his affection.

March 7

We have been here in the New World near four months and most of our number still live aboard ship. Work on the houses progresses slowly with all the illness. People are still dying. I still work part of the time in the Common House, helping. The elders will not let me near the sick, but I bring in a goodly supply of wood and tend the fire. Mrs. Hopkins does the cooking.

I have asked my master if I might learn to use a musket. He looked at me as if he did not know who I might be, shook his head in weariness, and said yes.

March 10

I have been training with the musket under Captain Standish. It is very tiring and not as easy as I thought. First, it is very heavy. I can scarce hoist it on my shoulder, but that it takes all my effort. I have struggled to learn the many steps to load it. Dotey and Leister are learning at the same time and hoist and do very well. Captain Standish says our services are needed as the Indians are still skulking around us. A man is posted to guard every night, and with so many sick we will soon be needed to take our turn. I hope I can acquit myself well when called upon.

March 11

We have had our first problem with discipline. Mr. Billington refused to take his turn at standing guard this past week. He asked why he should lose sleep for Indians who exist only in the tormented minds of the puke-stockings. "Do you see any Indians?" he bellowed at Captain Standish. For his disobedience he was tied neck to heels while all the company was made to watch. Mr. Billington was left that way for a few hours to mull the matter over in his mind. It was the sentence issued by Governor Carver.

March 12

The sun shines on us these days with more warmth than ever. The wind blows strong. But when it stops, I feel the first stirrings of spring. Some families have dug the ground and planted seeds in their lots, though their houses are not finished yet. My master's house is not yet finished. His wife still sleeps on the ship, and he works half the night taking care of the sick. I helped him do his planting. "Is this the first time you have put seeds into the ground, Jasper?" he asked me. I said yes. "I have done it many times, yet still ponder what a wondrous matter it is," he said. "You will see them grow. And someday you will have land of your own in which to plant seeds." Tom, I think that would even be more wondrous than seeing seeds grow.

There is talk that the *Mayflower* will sail within weeks. Captain Jones and the crew get restless. Elder Bradford looks around the board as we sup every night and asks, "Who amongst us hath died this day? And who is still with us?"

Thirteen have died this month. Scarce fifty of us remain.

Elder Bradford said two things as we sat at the board to eat this night. He said that if any amongst us wished to return to England when the *Mayflower* sails, he would not consider us beholden to him and we would have his blessing. Then he asked if anyone had any thoughts about how to lure the Indians to us. "We must start a discourse with them," he said. "We cannot continue to live in fear. If any of them make bold to come to you, lay down your musket and invite him to approach our settlement."

March 13

I write now in a corner of the Common House while the first grey light of dawn breaks outside. All around me the sick sleep with one or two attending them. I have just one candle to see. But I must write. Last night I stood guard for the first time! How fearful it was! How lonely! I stood on the edge of the settlement and walked around as I was instructed. Both Dotey and Leister have had their turns, and before I took my place they told me about the lions in the forest that they had heard. "They growled all night long," Leister said. "Be careful, wharf rat. Then there be the wolves. Their fangs drip. You are just the right size for them to devour in two bites. Their eyes glow red in the dark. And of course, the cloven-footed one roams, also looking for victims."

Though I paid no heed to them, when I was alone their words went round and round in my head. The sound of my own footsteps frightened me. I could see light through the small windows of the Common House, but it seemed so far away. What could I do if anyone attacked? Run? Yell? Would anyone hear me?

A waning moon was in the sky. I heard nightbirds, heard the waves breaking on the shore, heard rustlings from the forest. And yes, Tom, I heard the terrible howling of distant wolves. I calculated the time. I thought of all the clocks in Father's shop and how they used to tick, each with a different sound. Then chime all at once. We miss many things here, Tom, but every so often I think how much I miss the clocks.

As I made my rounds, the outline of the Hopkins house, the first finished, cheered me. I thought of Elizabeth Hopkins and the children safe in their beds. Of how she said I will grow and prosper in this land, and so will my children. But still I was sore afraid. The woods, Tom, the woods terrified me. I swear I could see forms in there, moving and keeping an eye on me. I heard voices. So, keeping in mind what Elder Bradford said about starting a discourse with the Indians, I set my musket upon the ground, faced the woods, and held my arms out as if to invite them to come and visit us.

Nothing happened. So hastily I picked up the heavy musket and recommenced my rounds, hoping no one saw me. But all the time I felt eyes on my back. I know they saw me. I just know it. And now I must put my book and pen aside and take my rest.

March 14

You will never guess what happened, Tom. I had finished carrying a load of wood to the fireplace in the Common House and was ready to sit down at a table for a meeting called by Captain Standish when there was a great commotion!

"Indians! Indians!" came the call from the man on guard outside the door. Such scrambling as I have never seen. We jumped to our feet, tripped over each other, grabbed for muskets, and if their intent towards us had been evil we would have been all dead. For no sooner did we raise our eyes than a savage walked right through the door and made bold to stand amongst us.

"Welcome," he said. Our mouths fell open. He spoke English! He was tall and of seemly carriage. He wore a quiver of arrows and carried a bow. We were seized with fear, for he was fearsome-looking. He wore but a fragment tied about his waist and the elders rushed to put a cloak around him. It was a red horseman's coat. He ran his hand over the buttons, nodded and smiled. "My name is Samoset," he told us.

Well, my bones were jumping, I can tell you. I was fearful and filled with excitement all at the same time. They invited him to sit. He nodded, but first asked for some beer. We had none so they gave him some strong water. Brandy. He drank it down and asked for more, which was given, along with biscuits and cheese, a bit of cooked mallard, brandy, and pudding. He ate it all.

"I have tasted this before," he said of the brandy. The elders asked him where. He said from English fishermen who had visited his country. Then he told us that he had been watching us for days, fearful to approach because of our big guns. But some of those who walked around looked friendly. At that utterance he looked in my direction, Tom, I swear to you. And smiled. I could scarce breathe. Had he, mayhap, seen me lay my musket down last night? I said nothing. Then he told us that he came from Pemmequid Point up the coast, where he was sagamore, or chief, of the Abnaki, who were called People of the Dawn.

They call this place where we live Patuxet. It means "little bay." The lord over all in his country, he told us, is Yellow Feather, also known as Massasoit. He is sachem of the Wampanoag and lives south of us on Narragansett Bay.

"He is lord over the warlike Nauset," Samoset told us. "They are a hundred strong."

He told us the reason no Indians had come to us is because this is the place of the Patuxet, who were all sickened unto death by the plague. The plague started at trading posts along the coast of Maine. "It is the burden of the white man," he said. "It killed whole tribes. There are no more Patuxet. Their skulls and bones lie in the earth."

He stayed for hours, Tom, telling us stories. We had no meeting. Night came and he made no move to leave, so the elders conferred. They must show him hospitality. But where? Then Mr. Hopkins looked at me. "Jasper, go to my house and ask my wife if it is agreeable to her that I bring this Indian home for the night," he said.

I saw in his eyes that he knew that his wife had the gift of second sight. And he knew that I knew it. And that if she said yes then we could be sure the Indian would not harm us. How does one gain such wisdom in a moment? I do not know. But I went to do Mr. Hopkins' bidding. None of the elders objected. I wonder, do they know she has the gift of second sight, too? Such matters are never spoken of among the Saints. Mrs. Hopkins said yes, bring the Indian. So I delivered the message and we all watched as Mr. Hopkins walked him across the compound to his home. Captain Standish asked for two guards to stand outside all night. I volunteered, Tom. Gladly. I could not have slept for the thoughts racing through my head.

March 15

There was no disturbance during the night. But how I envied Dotey and Leister, who slept in that house! Mrs. Hopkins came to the door this morning, smiled at me, and sent Samoset out with some biscuits and beer in hand. Mr. Hopkins came out with Dotey and Leister, who looked prouder than peacocks as they escorted Samoset back to the Common House. "You are a good lad to keep watch, Jasper," she told me. I asked her if he made any trouble. She said he lay before the hearth with the red coat wrapped around him and slept like Oceanus. "He will bring us no trouble," she said. "He was sent to us to help us."

Captain Standish gave him a knife, a bracelet, and a ring and he left, saying he would be back.

March 16

Today is the Sabbath and I slept through worship, but no one thought wrong of me. I awoke to shouts and greetings outside. I ran out with my clothing in disarray and my feet bare to see Samoset with five more Indians. Samoset still wore the red coat. The others sported deer skins, leggings, feathers in their hair. One even wore a fox tail. They had black lines on their faces! I put my appearance to rights and helped set up a table outside and bring the victuals to the board. Elder Bradford does not want the Indians catching any disease here. The weather was most accommodating and the Indians ate liberally.

After eating, the Indians stood and without further ado commenced to sing and dance. At first we were startled and moved away. They sang in their own language, though it was more like Popish chanting. They danced after the manner of lunatics. Elder Bradford scowled, watching. Dancing is a sin to the Saints, and since it is the Sabbath, the sin was twice as offensive. After the dance was over, they took from a basket some tools and beaver skins and set them on the table.

Mr. Hopkins recognized the tools as some stolen from the woods some weeks back when the men were cutting timber. The elders declined the beaver skins, saying they could not trade on the Sabbath, but they should return another time with all the beaver pelts they had and good trading would be accomplished.

The other Indians left, but Samoset stayed. He asked to sleep in the Common House. Elder Brewster warned him of the sickness there. Since there was no place to put him, I brought him to a house that was finished but empty. I also brought many blankets. "Welcome," I said to him.

He bade me to stay, so I did. "In the other wigwam the

elders are good," he said, "but the young men are trouble."
I knew he was speaking of Dotey and Leister. I nodded but
did not ask why. I do not know about Indians, but I sensed
he would not hold me in high esteem if I asked him to tell
tales. He then told me that they had many young men
like me back in his country. And if I visited I would be
welcome. We slept side by side in the empty house. I
cannot believe I have really spoken with an Indian, Tom!
Me! A waif from the streets of London! How can people
say they are savages? I felt comfortable and safe in his
presence.

March 17

We have spent the last few days hauling the goods from
the hold of the *Mayflower* to shore. Boxes and barrels and
crates, all to be dragged up the hill with ropes. Many boxes
were marked as belonging to Mr. Mullins, whose boot-
making shop was in Dorking. As I hauled the last of them
up the hill, Priscilla Mullins came to me shyly. "I need new
shoes," she said, then looked down at hers. Indeed they
were worn and muddy. "I know my father brought many
women's shoes. Could you find a pair for me?"

She is so pretty. Do you remember, Tom, the pretty
young maid who gave us sweetmeats when she came

with her father to have their clock repaired the last Christmas we had our shop? Priscilla is prettier than her. I could not deny her wish, though breaking into the boxes might bring punishment. John Alden, working nearby and seeing me bend to the task, came to help. In no time we found her a fine new pair of leather shoes. Tears came to her eyes as she held them against her. "My father made these with his own hands," she said. Then she thanked us and ran off.

They say Mr. Mullins brought twenty-five dozen pairs of shoes and thirteen dozen pairs of boots from England. In his will he left them to everyone in the company. Also he left forty pounds, and put in his will that Governor Carver and Mr. Williamson should keep an eye over his wife and daughter. I think that John Alden will soon make a move to keep an eye on Priscilla.

This evening Elder Bradford gathered all outside the Common House and gave to all who needed them shoes and boots.

Samoset stood on the edge of the crowd in his red coat, looking on. Without saying a word, Priscilla took up a pair of shoes with shiny silver buckles and brought them to Samoset. He took them and smiled. Other people gave him gifts, too. He left this night, with the shoes, some hose, a shirt, and a hat.

March 21

Again Captain Standish tried this day to have his meeting about military concerns. Again we were interrupted, this time by two fierce-looking Indians who appeared on Strawberry Hill. They made a semblance of daring by whetting the points of their arrows. Captain Standish and Elder Bradford put on their armor and muskets. Accompanied by two sailors from the *Mayflower* who had just brought ashore the last of the women and children, they made for the Town Brook and splashed across it to the hill. The Indians made horrible gestures and disappeared.

Captain Standish was newly concerned. Would we now have Indian trouble? We had our military meeting and made plans as to what to do in the event of an attack.

March 22

All are ashore now. I have thought that before the *Mayflower* sails I would like to walk her decks once more. This day again we were startled into action by the appearance of two Indians. But muskets were quickly laid aside when they turned out to be Samoset and a friend named Tisquantum, who calls himself Squanto. Samoset was greatly excited. The great chief Massasoit and his brother Quadequina were coming to see us!

We waited, and within the hour appeared on Strawberry Hill a force of Indians as would send us racing back to the *Mayflower* if we did not have leaders of great courage.

Quadequina was painted with bold colors on his face and arms. With him he had some sixty men, also making a most fierce appearance. Captain Standish murmured that if they were intent on trouble, their force was three times ours.

All were very worried. Samoset stood with them now and gestured that we should come and visit. Captain Standish declined and yelled that they should come forth and present themselves. But no side moved. Then Edward Winslow, who just lost his wife and who is but five and twenty, offered to approach them. With him he took a knife and a jewel for Quadequina to hang in his ear. We watched them from afar, not knowing what was transpiring but knowing that Samoset was acting as interpreter for Quadequina and Massasoit. There was much hand waving and loud talk. Finally Samoset came forward with Massasoit and twenty warriors. All their faces were painted in fierce colors, though they left their bows and arrows behind. Winslow stayed with the other Indians.

I wondered how Winslow felt, alone there on Strawberry Hill surrounded by those fierce warriors, who could kill him at any moment if they took a fancy to it.

Massasoit is very tall and stately. His body is oiled. He wears paint of a sad mulberry on his face. Others wear yellow, black, red. They are all taller than our elders. The first thing Captain Standish did was put himself at the right side of Massasoit, and with his men, including me, following, we marched him down our one street as women and children stood about staring. I was so proud to be included!

Where were we going? Captain Standish led us to a house yet in the building where a green rug was placed with some cushions. Governor Carver came with two of our men, one banging a drum and the other blowing a trumpet. Carver kissed Massasoit's hand and the warrior kissed him. Strong water was brought. Meat was served. Massasoit drew out a pipe from a bag. I stayed in the corner of the unfinished house, hoisting my musket on my shoulder for over an hour. I thought I would drop from weariness, but I was intent upon listening, Tom.

They drew up a treaty. When I saw it later, it had seven clauses. Here they are, as brief as I can write. First: They should not injure us or do hurt to any of our people. Second: If they did do hurt, Massasoit should send us the offender so we could punish him. And if we did like harm to them, the same should be done. Third: If they took our tools he should cause them to be restored. Fourth: If any tribes did unjust war against him we would aid him. If any did war against us, he would aid us. Fifth: He should send to his neighboring confederates to certify them of this. Sixth: When their men came to us they should leave behind their bows and arrows. And when we came to them we should leave behind our muskets. Seven: If they did all this, King James would esteem him as a friend and ally.

But it was not yet over. I was delighted to be asked to be in the company to escort them back across Town Brook, but all did not let leave. Quadequina, Massasoit's brother, insisted on being entertained in kind. He came back with many more men and we were obliged to give them strong water and meat. They left at dusk. Squanto and Samoset stayed.

March 23

As morning broke they came back, some with wives and children. They wished to be honored and entertained. Elder Bradford said we should all go about our work and pay them no heed, and they would leave. They did, but a message came later that our leaders should go their camp. Oh, how I wish they would go and mayhap take me with them!

March 24

Only Captain Standish and Isaac Allerton went. They returned today with a large kettle. Our elders filled it with English peas and sent it back to the Indians.

March 29

We have been most successful in our discourse with the Indians. Betimes we think too much so. There is much disorderly coming to our settlement of Indians, their wives, and children. They ask for food and strong water. They come at all hours, even in the middle of the night. Elder Bradford and Captain Standish said a mission must go to them and stop the nuisance visits. Along the way the party is to go to Sowams, whence comes Samoset, so we will know the way if the necessity arises for us to go for aid.

Mr. Winslow and Mr. Hopkins are named to the mission. Mr. Hopkins needs a servant, but would not take Leister or Dotey. Squanto did not wish it. He pointed to me. I was honored, yet frightened at the same time. Because now Dotey and Leister will have more reason to hate me. I am to carry the food, the water, the copper chain, and the red coat they desire to give to Massasoit.

April 3

We traveled two days, seeing many new sights. Sandy soil, marshes with tall grasses, places of sparkling ponds, tall pines, fowl and deer and beaver in abundance, fertile soil, small sweet brooks. Truly this land goes on forever, and in the sweet April air it looks the nearest to heaven I shall likely ever see. We arrived at our destination only to find that Massasoit was away. A runner was sent to fetch him.

We camped for the night. The next day the chief arrived. Hopkins and Winslow fired their blunderbuses in greeting. All the Indians in the village ran screaming in fear, but Winslow, with his soft words and diplomatic ways, soon quieted them and gave out the presents. "We being yet strangers at Patuxet, and not knowing how our corn may prosper," Winslow told the chief, "cannot yet entertain your people as we would desire. So we ask you to hinder the multitude from oppressing us with themselves."

Winslow then asked if they wished to trade some of their seed corn so we might see which kind we could best grow. It was agreed. We stayed the night, though were sorry to have done so.

They offered us no food, but Massasoit bade us share the royal couch with him and his wife. The royal couch turned out to be heavy timber logs with only thin mats over it. I slept on the edge and fell off twice. Lice and fleas were abundant and the savages sang all night. In the morning we left, hungry and scratching, but with a promise from Massasoit to leave Squanto with us to show us how to plant and otherwise survive. They also promised to come with beaver pelts.

April 4

Squanto came home with us. On the way he told us that he had been carried to England in 1605 by a Captain Weymouth and had come back to America in 1614 with Captain John Smith. When Smith left, one of his ships remained with a Captain Hunt who was ordered to load her with fish and beaver skins. Instead, Hunt loaded the ship with Indians and sailed away to sell them as slaves. Squanto and twenty from Patuxet and some from Nauset were taken.

They were sold at a slave market in Spain. Squanto and some others fell into the hands of friars, who wanted to make Christians of them. Somehow Squanto managed to sail away to London. There he lived with a rich merchant for several years.

Tom, he lived in London at the same time as us! He left for home in 1619, a year before the *Mayflower* set sail for America! He stayed awhile in Monhegan, the leading fishing station of Maine, and arrived in Plymouth Harbor just six months before we did! All his people were gone, carried off by the plague.

Now I know why Elizabeth Hopkins said Samoset was sent to us.

After we arrived home this day I bathed to rid myself of fleas and received permission to sail in the shallop this evening for a last visit to the *Mayflower*. She sails on the morrow. I climbed the ladder to board her with the strangest feeling. I once lived on this ship, shivered on her, starved on her. But she looked so different! All signs of our passage were gone. Sailors were swabbing her decks, which gleamed in the sun. Her masts were all mended. I went to the Great Cabin, where we stayed, and looked about. The emptiness was eerie. I felt a fondness for her, Tom, this brave sweet ship that brought us over the ocean to a new land. Then I heard someone behind me and turned to see Captain Jones. "Going home with us, lad?" he asked. I told him no, I came to say good-bye to the ship. He nodded and looked about, then back at me. "Few know that a ship has a soul," he said. "This one has a sturdy soul, and will be long remembered, though I be forgot."

I told him I would never forget him. Then asked him what his next port might be. He said he would find berth in the Thames River within a month. I then drew my book out of my pocket and asked him if he could have it delivered to the ship's chandler called Dorsey on Tower Street. He laughed and said he knew the man and would deliver it to him himself, that many on shore had asked him to bring home letters.

I told him it was for my brother Tom, who was supposed to sail on the *Speedwell* and was left behind. That Tom was likely still in Leyden with his master, Mr. Blossom, and mayhap Mr. Dorsey could send it to him.

He promised he would do his best. If you receive the book, Tom, be of good cheer. I am well and prospering. Elder Brewster tells us our children will say their fathers were Englishmen who came over the great ocean and were ready to perish in the wilderness to start this new land.

There should be more ships to follow us, Tom. Do come on one. Please. I wish you to partake of the plenty here in this place. And so I have handed my book to Captain Jones and now must try to find a new one. I hope I can. I shall ask my master.

April 5

My master hunted amongst his things and found a new book for me. The pages are so clean! Again I wonder what I shall end up writing on them. This is my first entry.

Today we all stood on shore and watched as Captain Jones brought the *Mayflower* around and tacked out of the harbor. On board his men fired their cannon in salute. Many of us cried. What a lonely group we seemed watching that ship sail away. But not one of our company went back to England with her. It is an act of faith, my master says, that all stay. I hope Captain Jones makes it back safely. His crew is near half in number because of sickness.

April 13

We plant. All dig and sow the seeds we have brought. In the lot of my master's house I drop turnip, cabbage, and parsnip seeds into the earth. It is so strange to look to the harbor and not see the sails of the *Mayflower*. I feel so alone. Others do, too, but speak not of it.

April 14

Priscilla Mullins has come to live under the roof of my mistress and master. All those made orphans this past winter have been taken into the homes of others. I cannot contain my joy! Besides being pretty, Priscilla brings lightness into our house. She helps Mrs. Brewster with the kitchen work and the washing. Our clothing is getting most shabby and she also helps restore it. At table she is free in speech and betimes makes us laugh, though on occasion a shadow crosses her face. Then she is remembering her parents. John Alden comes to call of an evening, now, and though weary from his work all day, he and Priscilla often sing at night.

Priscilla plays the dulcimer and they sing together. Sometimes Mrs. Brewster joins in. The songs are not psalms but merry songs once sung in England.

April 15

This day was hot. Heat must come early here in this place. We worked all day hoeing and planting and digging. About noon Governor Carver, who is neither a slouch nor ignorant of the hoe, came in from the common field wiping his face, which was very flushed. He complained of a pain in his head, went to his house, and lay on his pallet. About two in the afternoon his wife came out to tell us that he had become insensible to her. She could not rouse him.

April 17

There is a great heaviness amongst us at the loss of Governor Carver. He is mourned by both Saints and

Strangers. I was one of those who fired a volley of shot over his grave. His wife, Catherine, had to be held up at the ceremony. She mumbles about going back to Sturton le Steeple, whence she comes. But there is no ship to take her.

April 18

They speak of making my master governor, but he has no special eminence. My master says he does not envy the man who is picked, that his foremost duty will be to keep church and state separate here in this place. That the two mixing is worse than fire and gunpowder. All day he attended the meeting in the Common House to select a new governor. I spent the day working in the common field.

While I was so engaged, Squanto came along and stood watching me. "No way to plant corn," he said. And he came to kneel down and show me the right way. He made small hillocks with space between them. He told me how to tend and dress the plantings. Then he pointed to the Town Brook and said, "Come with me and bring your basket." So I dropped my hoe and went. He bade me to take off my shoes and hose and stand in the brook with him. So I did. And we waited. Finally I asked him what we were waiting for. "Alewives," he said. "They will come this day."

After a short time I saw swarms of alewives coming up the brook to spawn. Squanto bent over and caught them with his hands. I did so, too. In a short time he said we should go back to the common field. There he showed me how to set the fish as fertilizer on the corn. Three alewives must be placed, spoke-wise, with their heads toward the center on each hillock. And when this is done the common field must be guarded day and night against wolves. "Show the others," he said, "or you will starve next winter." Then he left.

At the end of the day, I knocked on the door of the Common House, and when told to enter I reported to the elders what Squanto had told me. They nodded. And all the young men were sent that evening to the brook to catch herring.

April 20

Elder Bradford has been elected our new governor. Dotey and Leister were set to guarding the common garden against wolves. I know they are not happy with me because I went in their stead on the mission to Sowams with Mr. Hopkins. Now they will be angry with me because I gave the information from Squanto that led to their long hours guarding the common garden.

April 22

Everyone is happy with the selection of our new governor. This day, as I was bringing in some wood for the Brewsters' hearthfire, Priscilla came out to speak to me. "There be trouble, Jasper," she said. She stood there wiping her hands on her apron. "When isn't there?" I asked. She smiled. "I would place my trust in you," she went on. So I said yes, do. Then she told me that she had become friends with Constance Hopkins, eldest in the Hopkins' household. Constance is fifteen. "Dotey and Leister both are enamored of her. And a rivalry is growing between them." I nodded, trying to be astute and solemn, even as my master would be. "And what of Constance?" I asked. "Does she favor one or the other of these fools?"

Priscilla sighed and shook her head. "She flirts with both. I have told her this will bring trouble, that both are hot-headed, but she continues to enjoy the sport of it."

"What would you have me do, Priscilla?" I asked. She said that mayhap I could speak with either Dotey or Leister. Or both. And warn them what trouble might occur. And I, a bigger fool than even Dotey or Leister, promised her I would. Because I did not want to seem of no eminence to this lovely girl who has so honored me.

But all I know is that if I do speak, they will have three reasons to be angry with me. And with their both being so hot-headed, it would take only two to get me killed.

April 25

A new Indian friend has come to live amongst us. His name is Hobomok. The Indians call him a pinese, which means he is a warrior of special courage and wisdom. He has been taken in hand by Governor Bradford, but I like him not. He wants to take the esteem from Squanto, who has taught us many things. Squanto would have left when Hobomok came, I think, if Captain Standish had not taken a special interest in him.

Now people say that Hobomok is Governor Bradford's man and Squanto Captain Standish's man. My master says we do not need to be divided like this. We need to work together.

April 28

Today I saw both Dotey and Leister walking with Constance Hopkins along the beach. She seemed very happy. I wonder if I should speak to Mrs. Hopkins about this? I wonder why this good woman, who has the gift of sight, does not see trouble coming in her own household?

April 30

We are all but finished with the planting, for which I am most thankful. Still, the common field must be guarded against wolves and my turn will come soon to guard it. And the garden in our own lot must still be tended each day. I bring water from the brook to water it, and hoe daily, too. Never did I think it took so much to bring forth food from the earth.

May 1

Some Indians came today to trade beaver skins. We have good relations now with almost all the tribes hereabouts except the Nausets. Squanto says they are the most war-like and cunning.

May 15

We have had much death here, many burials. Now we have had our first marriage. Mrs. Susanna White, a widow of three months, took unto her this day Edward Winslow, who lost his wife less than two months past. Governor Bradford performed the ceremony. It was not a religious ceremony but a civil one. The Saints say that marriage is a civil thing.

May 21

Summer is full upon us. Birds sing, the woods and fields are lush, the gardens grow, the sun is warm. Our men walk at peace in the woods and fields. We have eleven houses finished. They line both sides of our main street, which is a cannon shot of about eight hundred feet leading to the sea. We now have four buildings for common use, even a storehouse. The summer looks both promising and peaceful. It is important that the corn grow, for we have promised eighteen thousand guilders to our backers in London.

May 23

How wrong I was to think of peace. Today was my day to guard the common field. If I see wolves I am to fire a shot to bring help. I was walking my post when Dotey and Leister came by, taunting me. The day was hot and I was most uncomfortable and wished some water. They had some, but poured it out on the ground in front of me. "Serves you right, wharf rat, for boasting of what you knew to the elders. If you had kept a still tongue in your head, we wouldn't be here," Dotey said. "I have served twice to your once. And Leister three times." They then walked amongst the infant rows of corn.

"Have a care," I admonished. "It goes at three guilders the bushel. It will be sent in sloops to the north to be traded for beaver pelts with the savages to satisfy our debts to England."

"Listen to the little wharf rat," Dotey said. "Thinks he knows it all. Well, what do you think would happen if we just dispersed a few ears of corn here. And here." And so saying, he kicked at a row with his foot. I yelled for him to stop. But before I could advance on him he had ruined half a row. "Now you will be blamed," he told me. "And your master will have to make up the loss from his own garden. And you will be flogged, wharf rat. And next time you won't be going on any special missions in our stead, will you?" This from Leister. And then they ran. But not before apprising me of how dead I would be if ever I caused them trouble again. "Matters can be blamed on the Indians, you know," Dotey yelled as they ran through the woods. "A beaten body found on the end of the settlement. Who is to know?"

I stood ready to cry. Half a row of corn ruined! How could they be so dastardly? Whence had Mr. Hopkins gotten these jackanapes? I set down my musket, which I was cautioned never to do on guard, and went about restoring the kicked-over ears. I put most of them back in the ground, hoping the roots were not ruined. I covered over their mischief. And, by determining not to let any-one know of the incident, made some of my own.

May 26

This afternoon when I was readying myself to fetch water from the brook for my master's garden, Priscilla came to me. "Jasper, you must do something! I just spoke with Constance and she said that Dotey challenged Leister to a duel!"

I stared at the girl as if she were the spawn of the devil himself. "A duel? Are they mad?"

"They meet on the beach tomorrow at first light! It is so, Jasper! And it is over Constance!"

"Why doesn't she go to her mother or father?"

"She is most fearful of punishment for her part in it. She encouraged both and is interested in neither. Oh Jasper, please do something. You promised!"

I looked at her pretty, flushed face. I would no sooner go near Dotey and Leister now than I would go near a barrel of open gunpowder with a pine knot torch in hand. But she looked so distressed. Her eyes begged. Her breath was spent. "I will," I promised. "I will." When she asked me what I would do, I told her not to worry her pretty head. I sounded quite like John Alden and was most pleased with myself. But what I will do I do not yet know.

May 28

I am so weary now I can scarce write the last in this book
that I may write for a while. I must run now for my life,
and write so you will know, Tom, what happened to me if
I do not return.

All late yesterday I worried the matter of Dotey and
Leister. I decided I could not go to anyone in authority,
lest they be only boasting of dueling and I bring their
wrath down upon me. I would wake early, before first
light, to see if they creep out of the Hopkins house. Catch
them at it. See if they head for the beach, then go inside and speak with Mrs. Hopkins, who will be first up,
getting breakfast for her family. That was the only plan I
had.

I lay awake most of the night, fearful I would not wake
on time. I dozed and woke to hooty owls calling, to the
howling of a wolf, to a nightbird's call. Finally, when I saw
the first gray lightness in the eastern sky, I got out of bed,
dressed, and crept down from the loft, shoes in hand, and
out the back door.

It was not far to the Hopkins' house, and I stayed behind a fence, waiting. Sure enough, there was a light, a
small lantern in the hand of someone as the door opened.
And there were Dotey and Leister, creeping out onto the
street. Dotey carried a sword, likely stolen from his master.

Leister carried a long dagger. I followed them, staying a safe distance behind. I followed them far enough to see them make for the beach.

I ran as fast as I could back up the hill. What if they killed themselves in the meantime? I would be to blame. My breath spent, I approached the Hopkins house to see a light in the window. Mrs. Hopkins was awake! Thank the Lord! Gently I tapped on the door. When it opened, I spilled out the whole story. As she listened I saw Constance in her long white nightdress behind her mother. And Mr. Hopkins struggling into his doublet. "What goes?" he asked. So I told him, too.

Before we reached the beach we heard the clinking of sword against knife. Doors on the street were opening and people rushing out. Men had muskets in hand. Captain Standish was soon with us, told of the trouble as we proceeded on our way.

We got there just in time to see Leister down, with Dotey's sword piercing his thigh. He was moaning and cursing and slashing back at Dotey with his dagger, making gashes in Dotey's hand and forearm. Captain Standish was on them in an instant, along with Mr. Hopkins, drawing their own swords and demanding they cease this madness.

There was blood all over the sand. Women came rushing forward, offering strips of apron to bind up wounds. Captain Standish and some other men dragged them up the beach, Standish all the while yelling about what a foolish risk of life this was when we needed all able-bodied men to mayhap fight Indians. The culprits were bandaged and brought this day before Governor Bradford, who delivered a lecture and pronounced a sentence.

On the morrow they are to be strung up with head and heels tied together to cool off their hot blood. As they were taken away under guard Leister growled at me. "Your doing, wharf rat. You had better be ready for an Indian attack. It is coming."

Everyone thought he was out of his head and paid no mind. But I know better. So I know I must get away from this place now before they kill me. I packed some dried apples and bread in a sack. I have a flask of water. And this night as my people sleep, I will slip out the door.

May 29

I write in this book to anchor myself to the world. I sit alone by the fire, I know not where. I think I have stayed on the right path all day, but I am so tired I am not sure.

I left our village before anyone stirred about this

morning. The only person I saw was Mrs. Hopkins at the common oven, baking her bread. I knew it was her by the red shawl that she wraps around herself betimes to ward off the chill, but I was a hundred yards from the common oven at best count and dared venture no closer. I could smell the cooking bread. I knew she would give me a loaf if I asked, but I feared my own tongue. The lady sees so much, she would surely know I am running off. And I could not put that burden on her. She has enough burden now with Constance, who caused the duel between Dotey and Leister.

So I waited for her to lift a tray of small loaves and walk toward the house with them before I dared go near the common oven. Of course I put my hand inside to see if anything was there. I burned my fingers, but it was well worth the effort, for I came out with a small loaf, hot to the touch. I put it inside my doublet and ran off.

I headed then towards the woods, wishing I had a compass. But I knew where I was going. To Sowams. Had I not been there before? I knew the way. Hadn't Samoset said I would be welcome there any time? Of course he was not here, but I could not stay. So, sack in hand, I set off, confident of my way.

The woods were yet quiet, though birds were stirring and some small animals moved about. I wished I had taken my musket, but I could not. That would be stealing. It belongs to Captain Standish. I wished I had a knife, but I had not even that. No worry. I would be at Sowams in two days. My shoes were strong, my clothing worn but still sturdy and my head clear. I would make it.

All day I made my way through the woods. As I remembered my last trip, we did not stay to the woods, but betimes went through clearings. I could not chance being seen. By either my own people or Indians.

By midmorning I had seen two foxes, three snakes, and a dozen or so deer. How I wished I had the means to kill a deer and bring it as a gift to Sowams. It is always better to visit the Indians with a gift. I had none. I had not thought of that, nor did I think what I would do when I got to Sowams. Would they let me live there with them a while? At least until the anger of Leister and Dotey cooled down? Yes, that was it, I would ask them to let me live there for a while.

I traveled all afternoon. My legs hurt. My feet hurt, and just when the sun was making its farewell, I ventured out of the woods. All was swamp grasses and water, yet not the ocean, not the bay, and not a river. Just becalmed water. I recognized none of it, but decided I'd been too busy on the last trip to take note of landmarks. I gathered wood and built up my fire. Thank the heavens I had brought flints. I knew I would have to stay up all night to keep it going or risk being attacked by wolves.

I haven't brought a blanket either. How did I know the night would grow chill near the water? The days are so hot now. I huddle as close to the fire as I can and watch its sparks flame up into the night. It has become my whole world, that fire. I think about home. They would miss me by supper. I hope they will not send out search parties. 'Twould be a waste of time. I look up into the night sky. A quarter moon hangs over the water. From the forest comes the sound of wolves. There is no worse sound this side of hell than wolves when you are alone at night. I write in my journal to keep awake. I am all alone on the edge of the world. I am so lonely as to feel as if my soul has a hole in it and all my being is leaking out of me like water out of a barrel.

Later: I write in strange surroundings, but I write. Pain shoots through my legs and my head is throbbing and dizzy, but I write.

Twice I have dozed off. Did I sleep? Did I dream? I know I heard voices. Dotey's and Leister's, threatening me. I saw the lovely face of Priscilla, heard Captain Standish shouting commands. "Anyone who sleeps while on guard will be punished!" He drew me awake. Where was I? Then I fixed my gaze on the fire, like on the North

Star, and remembered. I got up, put more wood on the fire, and saw eyes a distance away, at the edge of the woods. Red, glaring eyes watching me. The Evil One! He had come to claim me!

But I am still drugged with sleep. I pulled myself awake, reached for a big stick, and sat down again by the fire. No Evil One, only wolves. And as long as I stay awake and keep the fire going, they will not approach. I sit here shivering, not from cold but from fear. The wolves sit, too, waiting patiently.

How their eyes gleam in the firelight! How haunted their faces seem. I have never been this close to wolves. They are so different from dogs. They have a look about them of being the pursued and the pursuer all at the same time. They are lean and cautious. And they cannot seem to be still, but pace, then sit, then pace again. How long we have stared at each other I do not know, but they seem to be laughing at me, to be saying, "We can wait. We know you will fall asleep. And then we will be upon you."

I wish I had not come. I wish I was back in my small bed in the loft of the Brewster home, hearing the breathing of Elder and Mrs. Brewster, of Love and Wrestling and Priscilla Mullins below me. Why did I come? I would rather be beaten near death by Dotey and Leister than torn apart by wolves.

May 31

I knew warm sun was on my face, and I opened my eyes to see blue sky, the cold ashes of the fire, and no wolves. I had fallen asleep on guard duty! Unforgivable! Why had the wolves not eaten me? I scrambled to my feet and went to the edge of the water to wash my face to bring myself full awake. I reached into my sack for the last pieces of bread and apple. Then I looked around.

The quiet darkness of the woods mocked me. The long stretches of sand mocked me. I was turned around from my path of yesterday. Lost. I might as well admit it. But I knew I must go west. That was the direction I wanted. So I proceeded on, staying this day out of the woods.

I tramped all morning along the line of tall grasses and water. I saw birds I have never seen before, and stopped betimes to watch them. I saw one with long legs, like a man on the streets of London at fair time, on stilts. Gulls swooped and cried. The sky seemed to get bluer and bluer until everything before my eyes seemed painted, like the backdrop in the London theater where you and I had run errands for the actors, Tom. My heart lifted. I felt so free with no one to answer to, no one to call me to prayers or remind me to hoe the garden. The air smelled so good I thought I could eat it.

But then I got hungry, reached into my sack, and

found nothing, so I headed to the woods where I knew there would be at least berries. I searched for an hour or two until I found some very good ones and sat down to eat them. But then, upon recommencing my journey, I realized that my search for berries had taken me deep into the woods.

I looked around. I had lost the water and tall grasses. The woods went on thick and endless and I did not know which way to go. How could I be so stupid? I was lost for good now.

The rest of my day was spent walking through thick briars and underbrush, getting my face and hands scratched, stumbling, and wishing I had never ventured outside our village. Likely I will die here if the wolves don't get me first.

I wish never to be so alone again. And I would rather sleep beside a chimney in the worst London alley than in the middle of this terrible silent beauty around me. I long for a human voice, a friendly face.

June 1

I am awake early. I sit up to look around. I am in a long house that looks to be made of bent tree saplings, with two holes in the roof to let out fire smoke. I cannot think for a moment how I came to be here.

Then I remember. I fell into the hole, just like a fox or wolf, Tom. I came upon something tied in a small bit of rawhide on the end of a stick, over a hole. I knew what it was. Bait. Squanto had told me that Indians catch small animals this way. I was so hungry. Hungry as a fox or a wolf. I knew I could reach out to the end of the stick and retrieve whatever was in the rawhide. I remember reaching. Then falling through darkness, just like a fox or a wolf. I tumbled down into blackness. I recollect it all now as I write it down in my journal, which I found next to me when I awoke. My head hurts, my body hurts, but I must get it down, lest I forget. Who put my bag with my journal in it here next to me? Who brought me here? And where am I?

I remember more now. A fierce pain in my leg. Then waking to find I was thrown over the shoulder of a young man. "Let me down," I cried. But even talking hurt my head. And moving sent waves of pain through me.

He laughed. And I went unconscious again.

Again I awoke to find myself in an Indian village. A number of Indians surrounded me. They were tearing my leg into pieces. I yelled in pain. Someone was making me drink a bitter liquid, even while they held me down by the shoulders.

Yes, I remember now. How I slept and awoke again to darkness and a fire burning nearby. How my ankle throbbed. So it was my ankle, not my leg. Someone approaches. More later.

Later: The someone who approached me was my age or a bit older. His hair was long and tied in two braids. His body gleamed in the firelight. He wore only a breech clout. Around his neck, he wore a stone knife. A leather pouch hung from his waist. And from his back hung a quiver filled with arrows. It looked to be made from the skin of a fox.

He smiled. "I am Chonuck, nephew of Massasoit. I learned to speak your language from Squanto and Samoset. I must know it, since I wish to be a pinese when I am grown. I have special powers."

"What powers?"

He smiled. "They led me to you." That was all he would say.

I felt ashamed because he was so strong and sure of himself and I was not. "You found me in the hole," I said. "Like a dumb creature."

"The fox is not dumb," he told me. "A wolf is not dumb. It takes great cunning to outwit the fox and the wolf. Even they fall into the hole."

I remembered the wolves then and told him about them. "Why did they not eat me when I fell asleep?" I asked. "Because," he said, "I knew you were lost somewhere. I was in the forest. But I did not know where. Still, I protected you from them. Knowing such is part of my powers."

"Thank you," I said.

"Thank Kiehtan."

"Kiehtan?" I looked around for someone else to thank. But all others had left and I saw no one. "There is no one else here." He told me that Kiehtan is the Creator. That he is here, part of everything, though his habitation lay far west, in the heavens. "He made the earth, the heavens, the stars, the sea, and all the creatures," he told me. "All good men go to him when they die. Bad men go, too. They knock on his door, but to them he says, 'Quatchet,' which means 'Walk away. There is no place here for you.'"

"I thank Kiehtan then," I said, though I knew my elders would take fits if they knew I said it. "But I thank you, too." He told me that he should thank me, because I helped him prove his powers. "It is what I was in the woods to do," he told me. "I am learning from my uncle. And since you have helped me, I will be your friend for the next few suns. Whatever favors you wish, just ask them."

I asked him instead what a pinese was. He said it was a future war leader and adviser to a sachem. Like our elders? I asked. He said yes. Then I asked if this was his uncle's house. He said no. This was not Massasoit's village. That was a distance from here. This was a fine, two-fire house belonging to a sachem named Iyanough. This place was called Cummaquid.

My head was taken with dizziness. And I was hungry. But he had brought me a bowl. "Sobaheg," he said. I took it and ate. It was good. There was some kind of meat in it, I think, and green leaves. He watched me eat, then told me to rest, sleep. We would talk more later. "My sack," I said. "Thank you for saving my sack." He nodded and told me to rest. He would be by later. I have written down what befell me now, and lie back in weariness. I must sleep.

June 3

I did not write yesterday. As it turned out, I spent the whole day with Chonuck in the village. I met Iyanough. He was most kind and bade us stay a while and not go too far into the wood because of my ankle.

The two-fire house I was kept in had baskets and animal pelts hanging from the bent saplings inside. I lay on a raised bed. Wait until I tell my elders about all the pelts! And then I remembered. I will never see my elders again. I had run away. I felt a certain sadness, but then forgot it as Chonuck took me outside.

All around me people were working and children

were playing. I saw gardens, smaller wigwams, neat paths. A man was burning out the middle of a long log to make a canoe.

Several people looked up as I came out. The small children ran over to me and gazed up at me, saying something in their language and pointing and laughing. "Wautaconuoag, wautaconuoag," it sounded like. "They call you coat man," Chonuck said. "Would you like to go fishing?" he asked. I said I would.

They catch their fish in weirs, Tom. They drive stakes into the mud of the brook or pond, wide at one end and narrowing at the other, which is upstream. The fish swim, in schools, through the narrow opening into a square of close-set stakes. They cannot escape. I spent all afternoon helping Chonuck make a weir.

The first thing he made me do was take off my shoes and hose. As we were working, it became so warm I soon took off my shirt. He laughed and said he would make a true Indian of me. I felt the sun on my back. The water of the stream made my ankle feel better. Of course, every so often I looked around and could not believe I was here, that I had run off. I thought about my people, our village. Had they missed me yet? Would they send someone looking for me?

For our noon meal, Chonuck took something out of the pouch around his waist and poured it into my hand.

It was dry. "Eat," he said. "It is nokake. Parched maize." I ate of it, expecting to choke. But it was good and filled my stomach.

I lost all track of time as we worked. I did not need time. We laughed and talked. He told me that everything has a spirit. Deer, bear, rocks, trees. That when the Wampanoags go hunting, they pray to the spirits of the animals to bring them success. And in turn the animals allow themselves to be caught. "But we do not offend them by killing more than we need to eat," he said.

When the sun was low we went back to the village with many fish. We ate around the fire with the others. Chonuck said that on the morrow we go to visit another tribe.

June 5

And so we did. We traveled for two days. I have shed my breeches now and my underclothes for a breechclout of animal skin, just like Chonuck. It is better, for the air is warm. As I stuffed my clothing into my sack I asked myself if I would ever have need of my English clothing again. I do not know. I do know that it is much faster to travel without shoes.

My ankle is better. Chonuck placed something around it that he said is the soft inner bark of a mountain ash tree. He said it would help the healing. He tied it with some sinew from a bear. He gave me, too, some trumpet honeysuckle leaves to chew. When I finished chewing I was to take the matter from my mouth and put it over the bites I got that day from insects. This is a bad season for insects, he says. But not as bad as August and September, which they call Micheennee Keeswosh, the time of everlasting flies.

The chewed leaves worked not only on my bites, but on my scratches. Then Chonuck gave me some bear fat to rub on my body. It would keep the briars from scratching me and the flies and mosquitoes from biting. He said that if my head hurt he had medicine for that, too. I think we could have used him on the *Mayflower* and during the first months after we landed. Mayhap not so many would have died.

On our two-day journey we did not hurry. We stopped to swim, to watch birds in flight, to bask in the sun. I am very brown now. I think I could be taken for an Indian. Never have I felt so free. There is no one to call me to prayer, no one to tell me to wash, no one to tell me I must do chores. I wonder, why don't we all live like this? Why do we bring so much work and guilt and sorrow down on ourselves?

This night, both taken with weariness, we reached the village of Massasoit. Everyone calls him Yellow Feather.

The village is on the shores of a large bay. It is even more beautiful here than where I come from.

There was much joy when we arrived. Everyone gathered around us and Chonuck spoke in his language, but I knew he was speaking of me and how he had found me. His uncle embraced him then and I saw that Chonuck had proved himself able to be a pinese.

We ate. Someone had trapped a deer and was roasting it over the fire. Massasoit then smoked a pipe with some of the other elders and passed it to Chonuck. I could tell this was his first time smoking, because he choked and laughed. They did not pass it to me, for which I was grateful. My skin burns as if the sun were still upon it. Yet I seem to have chills. My head hurts, and I wonder if I will lie down and die like Governor Carver. "I must write," I told Chonuck. He said write, yes, do, so I took out my journal, quill, and ink. They all came close then to watch. I think they have never seen a coat man writing before. Chonuck said they thought it was magic. And that since he saved my life this added to his powers. He was very pleased. But soon my head hurt and Chonuck gave me a worn skin. His mother came to me and gave me a drink of strong herbs and spoke sharply to him.

In summer they do not sleep in the wigwams if the weather is fair. So we took our blankets and found a quiet place and went to sleep.

June 6

When I woke I felt better. Chonuck gave me a bow and a quiver of arrows. "Today we hunt," he said. So we made ready to leave the camp. Just then Massasoit came to us and spoke to his nephew in their language. There seemed to be some disagreement, and I thought we would not be allowed to leave, but we did. This, I thought, is one reason I would like to be an Indian. Chonuck can do as he pleases. My spirits were greatly uplifted. My head was clear, my skin no longer burned. The skies were blue, the wind fair, and the day high with promise.

We went to the woods. Once there in the cool shadows, Chonuck told me his uncle had received word that my people were searching for me. "He says that as sachem of all the Wampanoag, he must tell them where you are. He said he will send runners today to bring word to your people that you are safe."

I told him I did not wish for this to be. I did not wish to go back to my people. He was most solemn. "My uncle made a treaty with your people," he said. "He considers it his duty as part of that treaty to let them know where you are. Or it could be taken that my people hold you as a hostage."

I would have to go back to my village and face Dotey and Leister. "Do not look so sad," Chonuck said. "You know you must go back to your people. And we have this day together."

And we recommenced to walk. "Where are we going?" I asked. He answered, "My uncle wishes me to take you to the nearest village of the Nauset."

Well, I stopped dead in my tracks, Tom. "They will kill me," I said. "They are the enemy of the white man. Squanto, Samoset, even your uncle told us this." He said yes, that was true, but think of how wonderful it would be if I bring them and your people to a council fire, to a treaty. It would be peace, as my uncle promised.

"But suppose they kill me first?" It was all I could think of. "Suppose they don't like me and kill me? Or take me prisoner?" This they will not do, he said. I asked him how did he know. And he said, "Because I have powers to be a pinese. I can bring them to welcome you."

"You are not a pinese yet," I reminded him.

"Do you not believe in me, then?" he asked. "Did I not keep the wolves from devouring you?" Again I looked in those brown eyes. "I believe in you," I said. "I do not believe in the Nauset."

So he showed then the wisdom that will make him a pinese. He asked me if I did not wish to be in good standing with my people. I said I always wished to be looked upon as doing something good, but never could accomplish this. "Won't they be angry with you for running?" he asked. I had not thought of that. He was right. They would be. "But if you go with me to the Nauset, and they favor you as the other tribes did, and you bring about peace, will not that put you in good standing?"

He was right, of course. "I will go with you," I said.

He said, "Good. But first you will have a day you will always remember. When you sit by the fire when you are an old man, you will remember this day, I promise you."

And true, Tom, I shall always remember this day. The sky touched the earth in whatever direction we went. All creation seemed like one. The sun shone, but did not burn me. The wind, filled with salt air, was my friend and seemed to whisper to me, "Look, look, now. See everything." I learned to use my arrow and felt as if it was Gideon's sword. I heard the sound of brooks and knew it was the sound of my own blood. We ate berries of a kind I had never tasted before. We swam. We caught and cooked fish. We explored like children. We heard birds such as I have never heard, the squeak of opossums. We even saw a bear. We ran through meadows so stark with beauty and freshness that I knew no man had run through them before.

We went into swamps, which I told Chonuck my people think bad, the harbinger of the Evil One. He said swamps are good places, they house good spirits, they welcome you. We saw mallards, turtles, snakes, deer, beaver, a cloud of pigeons. Chonuck told me about them all. We shot our arrows into a flock of partridge and got one. Then, as the afternoon waned, we stood and watched the sun set, dipping redder and redder into the earth.

Never have I felt so alive. Never have I felt the closeness of the earth before. Always I had considered nature a thing apart from me, a thing to fear, to protect myself against. Now I know it is part of me. My skin told me, my blood and eyes told me, my nose and the soles of my feet told me.

June 7

We made camp for the night, made a fire, and cooked some fish and pigeon. I am very happy.

June 8

As the sky was streaked with the red and gold of sunrise, more beautiful than anything I had ever seen, we came to the Nauset village. Many people were awake already, of course. Smoke rose out of the tops of the lodges.

When we first walked into the village, they did not know I was not an Indian. How could they? I was dressed like Chonuck. I carried a bow and quiver of arrows, my limbs and chest and face were browned by now from the sun. They greeted us. Or more rightly, they greeted Chonuck, and I stood back, a little frightened. These are the people who would kill me, I thought. Chonuck presented them with the partridge we had shot. A gift.

Then someone took note of me, of my eyes, which are blue, and started chanting, "Wautaconuoag! Wautaconuoag!" Which I knew by now was coat man. Before I knew what was happening, they were dragging me off to a chief who had yellow and black stripes on his face and who looked more fierce than the Evil One himself. I yelled for Chonuck, but the Nauset had me surrounded.

The chief they called Aspinet scowled down at me and asked questions of the two warriors who held me. They spoke in words of a horrible language. Or mayhap it was not the language, but the tone. They pointed to Chonuck. Aspinet nodded, then reached out to touch me. I shrank from his touch, but his men held me. He looked into my eyes. He touched the quiver of arrows on my back. He took my small sack and drew out my shoes and clothing and threw them on the ground. He took up my journal, my quill, and my ink. He held the small bottle up to the sun as if to get some message from the contents. Then he rifled through my journal, grunted, and gave me a most terrible look and demanded something of me. But I could not understand what he wanted. Where was Chonuck? Was this a trap? Had he betrayed me?

I looked around, but he was nowhere in sight. Aspinet made the same demand again. I shook my head no. I did not understand. So his men dragged me off to a small wigwam where they tied me to a pole.

I could not see at first in the darkness, but when my eyes accustomed themselves, I saw the same pelts and baskets hanging here as I'd seen in other wigwams. Yet I could not turn my mind to them. Outside there was still shouting. Excitement. Anger. Then silence. I stayed there for a long time tied to that pole, Tom, knowing they were going to kill me. Either Chonuck had betrayed me or his powers did not work here. I thought about you, across the ocean. I thought of the clock shop, of father, even of our tutor. I thought of the richness of London's streets and how I would die here in this forsaken place, tied to a pole with dust and hate all around me. I thought of all the burials I had attended in our village and how they'd likely leave my body to rot in the sun.

The flap opened and one of them came in with my sack. He threw it at my feet and left. I kept looking for Chonuck to come in, but he did not. How could I have been so stupid? What did we really know about the Indians and their ways? I became angry, then. I was an Englishman! They could not treat me this way.

I began to be sorry I had left the village.

The day went on. Flies buzzed around me and I could

not brush them away from my face. I was thirsty and I had to make water at the same time. If they were going to kill me, I wished they would just get it over with. Then the flap opened again and one of the men who'd brought me in came to untie me. I dropped to the ground, exhausted. "Kill me now," I said. "Please." I decided to be brave, at least. I had heard somewhere that Indians hate cowards. But I knew fear, Tom. Worse than any inspired by Dotey and Leister. "Where is Chonuck?" I asked the warrior who had come in. But he only left again. I was untied but still captive. I determined not to run. Mayhap they were waiting outside for me with pointed arrows.

In a little while the same warrior came back in with a bowl. In it was water. He pointed to my sack, then to the bowl of water, which I wanted more than I wanted to live right then. I picked up the sack. He nodded and grinned. I took out my journal. More nodding. I took out the quill and ink. He became so glad then I thought he would dance for me. But instead he gave me the water. I drank it down like a sailor drinks beer after a storm at sea, Tom. Again more pointing to the journal and to me.

Then I understood. He wanted me to write! But what? They could not read or write. Nevertheless I started writing this account thinking of you. It calmed me and he squatted down watching and grunting his approval. Then when I wrote a bit he bade me stop and rise. I covered the ink bottle and got up. He gestured that I should take bottle, quill, and journal with me and led me out of the wigwam into the gathering dusk.

There were fires burning. I smelled food cooking, saw women bending over pots and stirring. I was reminded of how hungry I was. But Aspinet stood waiting for me. As they led me to him Chonuck came over, smiling at me. "Where were you?" I asked.

"You had to face them alone. They wanted it so. You had to earn their approval without me."

"If you knew this, you could have told me," I scolded him. He nodded and smiled again. "Then there would have been no approval for you to earn. Now I will tell you, they want you to write." I told him I knew that, and I asked him what. And why. He said it did not matter. They were taken with the journal, with the words on the paper, they said the words looked like blackbirds flying. They thought it was magic and they wanted me to write for them and tell them of this magic. He said he would translate.

So we sat down, Tom, and I wrote in this journal, which has likely saved my life. I am writing this last entry while Aspinet and others watch. We told them I was writing for you, the brother who lives across the great sea. They nod their approval. Chonuck translates. I tell them about King James and how he burns women for witches and throws people into prison for thinking for themselves and how we had gotten on a boat and crossed the ocean to find our own place, away from him. I tell them how terrible the voyage was.

They have just brought me food in a bowl and a string of shells to wear around my neck. Aspinet has told Chonuck that he will meet with my people. That any people who did this were worthy and should be met with.

June 12

Tom, I am back home. How strange it is. I walk the streets of Plymouth and everyone smiles and waves at me. I am the Boy Who Made Friends With the Nauset. When our elders came to rescue me, they came in a shallop with Iyanough, the sachem of the village where we stayed the first night, two of his braves, and Squanto. The elders had sent messages to the Indian villages asking after me. They had given me up, thinking I had been eaten by wolves, when the runner came from Massasoit telling them of my visit.

At first when the elders came seeking me, they would not disembark from the shallop. Night was coming on and the beach was crowded with Nauset who signaled that the white men should come closer. The tide was going out, and the shallop could get no closer to them. Or mayhap the fear of the elders prevented their coming. Finally, however, they brought the boat closer and I saw that Governor Bradford himself had come, but that he had men armed at the prow. This was bad, I thought. Then I turned and saw Aspinet with many braves, all bows and arrows at the ready.

Tom, I went to stand beside him so the elders could see that everything was all right. Chonuck stood with me. And when the elders saw this they waded ashore and were soon talking. I had changed to my regular clothing, not wishing to displease my elders, but I still wore the necklaces of beads and shells the Nausets had given me.

Then Aspinet walked me to Governor Bradford, stood behind me with his hands on both my shoulders, and pushed me to him and said something. Squanto translated. "They say the boy is of the greatest stature and strength," he said.

Tom, I near burst with pride. Governor Bradford smiled and gave him a knife and other gifts. They sat for a while by the fire and promises of peace were made. I said good-bye to my new friends, and to Chonuck. "You are under the special protection of the gods," he told me.

"You will never be wounded in a battle. I account it death for whosoever will try to harm you."

Later, when we were alone, Squanto told me that this is how they describe a pinese.

September 4

I have not written for three months. Our life improves here in this place. All summer I worked diligently to make up for running off. For, though my elders did not scold or punish me, they did indeed remind me of the fear I had put upon them. "Peace with the Nauset came from your actions," my master told me. "But there was no peace in our hearts when we learned that you fled. We are a company of people of one thought and mind here, Jasper. We work for the good of all. Would that you had come to me with your fears and let me allay them." I promised him that next time I would.

The elders decided, in my absence, to make wine. The wild grapes, both red and white, are in abundance here in this place. And they have no beer. The harvest has been good. We have onions, carrots, parsnips, cabbage, beets, and radishes and much more. Squanto's direction for planting worked well. Under his eye I planted pumpkins in the middle of the corn, which he has taught us to cook over the fire coals in earthen jars until it pops and makes fluffy balls. One day he gathered all the women near the common oven and taught them how to make pudding. He put cornmeal and molasses in a pouch and boiled it in water.

With so much abundance, our elders have decided to have a day of thanks. Elder Bradford said that it should be custom to celebrate the harvest as they did in the homeland. So we now prepare for the day.

I have been sent out with a party of men to hunt waterfowl. Massasoit is invited. I look forward to seeing Chonuck again. Tom, how I wish you were here to partake of this celebration with us.

September 15

The celebration was a great success. Our hunting party brought back enough to furnish the whole colony with food for a week. Massasoit brought ninety braves. And Chonuck. We had a fine time, playing games and eating. The Indians did not leave for near a week.

November 9

Priscilla Mullins and John Alden are courting. Mistress Hopkins made a special corn cake for my fifteenth birthday. "Oh, Jasper, I feel so ashamed," she told me. "I have the gift of second sight, yet I could not see trouble brewing in my own house. I have sinned in my pride and the Lord punished me." I told her the Lord would never punish her if she could make corn cake like she did. And she laughed. I think forever we will be friends.

December 9

This day as my master and I were repairing some chinks in the house to ready it for winter, an Indian came running into the village. A ship had been spotted off Cape Cod. "A canoe with tall sails," he told us. All went running because at that moment the cannon on Fort Hill boomed. When we arrived there, Captain Standish ordered "every man, yea, boy, that can handle a gun to make ready." And we did so. Captain Standish said he feared it was a French vessel down from the Canadian settlements. And that being the case they would surely try to raid us.

But oh, the joy when the ship hove in sight and its captain ran up the ensign, upon which was the red cross of England on white. We had not been expecting a ship so soon. She was the *Fortune*, a ship of fifty-five tons. Thirty-five souls were on board.

We went to meet them. There was Jonathan Brewster, my master's son, a widower of thirty years. There was a youth of nineteen called Philippe de la Noye, who, upon setting foot on shore, declared that henceforth he would be known as Delano. There was a carpenter, a miller, and a woman schooled in the art of teaching.

It is good to have new people here in our village, though they brought not so much as a bisket-cake with them. They have not brought many pieces of clothing and are all hungry. "Still," my master said as he stood next to me, "their hands will be welcome as we start to build a palisade around the village. Look, Jasper, there's a likely lad who will be a help to us."

I looked. And there, there as my eyes squinted in disbelief, as my heart hammered and as my soul lifted to heaven, were you, Tom, who came ashore and squinted, freckles and all, with a face most impudent. "My master would not come," you said. "So I begged him to put me to Mr. Hicks, whose wife teaches. I wanted to be here in this place with you, Jasper. Your journal made it sound as if it is a place where all men in good standing should be."

He brought with him the first half of my journal, which I bind to the second half here in hand. I shall put it away, but keep it always. For I have come to be a man here in this place. And now I must help Tom to the same estate. There is much work to do.

Epilogue

Jasper Jonathan Pierce stayed on with Elder Brewster even after his indenture was over, working for wages on Brewster's farm across the harbor in Duxbury, or Ducksbarrow as it was then known, "the first of Mother Plymouth's daughters," meaning the first town created after Plymouth. Brewster's wife had died, as had his daughters Fear and Patience and his son Wrestling. His son Jonathan was off exploring Connecticut. Jasper ran the farm for him and was allowed use of his library.

Part of the reason Jasper stayed after his indenture was finished was to save money. Partly it was to oversee his brother Tom, who had yet to serve out his seven years to Mr. and Mrs. Hicks. There was no formal school yet in Plymouth, but Mrs. Hicks continued with Tom's education, being herself a teacher. And there were many nights when Jasper joined them around the fireside and shared what he knew from reading the books in his master's vast library.

When Elder Brewster died in 1643, he left Jasper a "milde, yet goodly sum" and a tract of land. By this time, Jasper was ready to wed and took unto him a likely lass named Jenny Souther, who came on the ship *Charity* in 1624. Jenny and Jasper built a house on his land, but both were still Strangers and soon the Saints owned and controlled the colony. Jasper had no vote in any weighty matters. The right to vote was restricted to freemen, who had to pass an examination of their religious views and moral character. Many a Stranger was "warned out" of the colony.

So Jasper and his wife moved to Salem (originally called Naumkeag). Shortly thereafter, he engaged in Indian and coastal trading and slowly amassed his own fortune. His brother Thomas and Thomas's wife, Patience, moved to Connecticut. Both soon had families — Thomas and Patience two girls, and Jasper and Jenny two boys.

When, in the summer of 1649, "infectious fevoure" spread through the countryside, Jasper lost his wife and two boys. Heartbreak followed Tom, also, when in the spring of 1637 an attack by Pequots on Wethersfield, his home, resulted in the slaying of six men, three women, twenty cows, and one horse and the capture of two girls, one Tom's.

Tom took part in the Pequot War of 1636–1637 against New England's Algonquians. While on a trading expedition to Maine in 1640 — which some say was really a mission to find his still lost daughter — he was killed by Indians.

Jasper married again in 1652, one Elizabeth Nutting of Salem. His son William became a respected merchant trader in that town and was among those who resisted the witchcraft hysteria in 1692. His other son, Resolved, born in 1657, became owner of a merchant ship. He sailed to Nova Scotia, trading corn for furs, and to Bermuda, the Netherlands, and British Isles to trade lumber, hides, masts, wool, salt, linen, hardware, and bar iron. He eventually became one of Salem's richest merchant traders.

Life in America
in 1620

Historical Note

After the arrival of the *Fortune* in December of 1621, the Pilgrims were still not free of worry of death or starvation. Although the *Fortune* and its thirty-five passengers provided joy, there were also concerns. The backers of this ship had sent the group out without "so much as a bisket-cake or any other victuals." Nor did they have any decent bedding, or, as Governor Bradford wrote, "but some sorry things they had in their cabins; nor pot nor pan to dress any meat in, nor overmany clothes." So, while the Plantation was glad of this addition of strength to their numbers and the talents they brought, they all wished the passengers had been better provided.

Another hard winter awaited them. Moreover, Mr. Weston had sent a biting letter scolding them for sending the *Mayflower* back without any cargo. So the Pilgrims worked long and hard to load the *Fortune* up with goods in payment to their backers before she weighed anchor and left.

When she departed on December thirteenth,

Bradford described her as "being laden with good clapboard as full as she could stow, and two hogsheads of beaver and otter skins gotten from Massasoit's men." The Pilgrims also had included some hardwood timber.

But on the way home the *Fortune* was captured by French pirates and her cargo was confiscated. Eventually released, the *Fortune* got to England with perhaps the most important item aboard, a written account entitled *A Relation, or Journal, of the Beginning and Proceedings of the English Plantation settled at Plymouth in New England*. The captain safely delivered it and it was published with the name of the author given as G. Mourt. Today it is available in pamphlet form and known as *Mourt's Relations*. It was written by Governor Bradford and Edward Winslow in what they called "a plain and rude manner." It was the first propaganda or public relations tract to come out of America. The elders of Plymouth were hoping for more settlers, and it was designed to attract as many people as possible.

After their first Thanksgiving feast, the Pilgrims worked hard all that winter. There was more Indian trouble in the form of threats from the Narragansett. And they decided to build a barricade to improve fortifications. Captain Standish reorganized their army into four companies with Bradford, Allerton, Winslow and Hopkins as commanders. Each of the four walls of the barricade was guarded by one company at all times. But they still had Squanto and the friendly Indians to advise and help them.

However, the Pilgrims had a couple of years of a disappointing corn crop, and though the fish were abundant, they still did not have the proper netting, tackle, or hawsers for their shallops. Indeed, at one point in 1622 they had to sail to the country of the Nauset and were supplied by Aspinet with beans and maize. Other foraging expeditions followed, and it was only the generosity of Cape Cod's friendly Indians that kept them alive during the first few years.

Then, in the spring of 1623, when starvation was still a very real threat, the elders decided to take a "contrary" step. Up until then all the corn had been grown in the common fields. Governor Bradford and other elders decided to allot acres for personal use and each household was granted land. This seemed to set every man to work "for his owne perticuler," and matters improved — especially when, in 1623, corn became a medium of exchange in the beaver trade.

"Greate cattle" did not arrive until 1624, when three heifers and a bull came for the use of the whole community. By 1627 many other ships and pilgrims had arrived. Now they had not only the means for fishing, but were growing grain, hay, and other produce. They had cattle, milk goats, oxen for plowing, and a steady trade going with the Indians for beaver pelts.

An essential note here: The peoples of Europe did not drink their water, since it was so contaminated because of poor sanitation. Following this tradition, the Pilgrims continued to make and drink their own beer in the New World.

By 1630 there were two hundred and fifty people living "without want, but without luxury" in Plymouth. By 1632, since more land was needed for arriving colonists and on which to keep cattle, they expanded to the north, distributing thousands of acres to land-hungry settlers. People began moving out of Plymouth, and new towns developed: Salem, Beverly, Scituate, Weymouth, Sandwich.

In 1630 John Winthrop arrived and soon departed from Plymouth with a large company of followers to settle Charlestown, and then Boston. Also in 1630, thirteen ships crossed Massachusetts Bay with a thousand new settlers, making for Winthrop's colony. Now Plymouth and the original Pilgrims were outnumbered, but their courage and influence had started the New World.

In 1643 a meeting was called at Boston to discuss an alliance of various settlements in New England, lest the Indians, French, or Dutch attack. The Articles of Confederation were signed by the colonies of Massachusetts Bay, Plymouth, Connecticut, and New Haven. In 1692, Massachusetts Bay obtained a charter from King

William and Queen Mary. The town of New Plymouth was included in the boundaries, as were New Hampshire and Maine. And so it was that the Old Colony ended after seventy-three years, absorbed into Massachusetts Bay Colony.

What of the "old comers," as the passengers of the *Mayflower* and *Fortune* began to call themselves? John and Priscilla Alden were wed in 1622 and had five children. They moved to Duxbury, one of the first towns established after Plymouth. Alden became assistant governor and died in 1687 at the age of eighty-nine, outliving many of his children. He was buried beside Priscilla on their farm.

Captain Miles Standish died in 1656 after years of being Commander-in-Chief of the small Pilgrim army. His oldest son married a daughter of John and Priscilla Alden. He left a large estate to his second wife, Barbara, and his children.

Six months later, William Bradford died, governor to the end. He was the richest man in the colony, with a three-hundred-acre farm. He is considered one of the greatest figures of seventeenth-century New England.

In 1644, Stephen Hopkins and Elder Brewster died. Brewster had lost his wife Mary, his daughters, Fear and Patience, and his son Wrestling. Though an elder, he continued laboring in the fields and as he grew older spent more time in his library of some four hundred books. Hopkins' wife Elizabeth died in 1640.

John Howland, the indentured servant who fell overboard on the *Mayflower*, inherited his master, Governor Carver's, estate and purchased his freedom. He married Elizabeth Tilley and was put in charge of the Kennebec trading post. He died in 1672, leaving nine children.

Edward Dotey served out his indenture, married twice, and died at Yarmouth in 1655, leaving nine children. Edward Leister went to Virginia "after he was at liberty" and there died.

Captain Christopher Jones died on March 5, 1622, and was buried in the churchyard at Rotherhithe, England. The *Mayflower* never sailed again after the death of her master and by 1624 was rotting away.

Squanto died in 1622, staying a friend to the Pilgrims all the while. Massasoit died in 1661. Upon his death, his eldest son, Wamsutta, succeeded him. When Wamsutta died in 1662, his younger brother Metacom succeeded him as sachem. The two had taken English names, Wamsutta calling himself Alexander and Metacom taking the name of Phillip.

It was Phillip who went to war in 1675 and 1676 in the first clash of the Indians and whites, which became known as King Phillip's War. Phillip and his men attacked many towns, sacking and burning and kidnapping. The war spread through New England. There was a heavy loss of life before Phillip and his tribes lost and peace was restored, and much of New England was devastated.

What was started with that group of Separatists in Leyden, Holland had far-flung effects for the world in years to come. How would those freezing, starving Pilgrims, carefully investigating the beaches of Cape Cod, feel to know they were establishing a foothold in what was to become the hope of the free world — America? Could they have guessed the immensity of their purpose, the wide-ranging results? One would think not until one reads their own accounts, which convey a God-driven sense of purpose. They seemed to know that they were building and starving and freezing not so much for themselves as for the good of future mankind.

Or, in William Bradford's words, "Yea, though they should lose their lives in this action, yet they might have comforte in the same . . . all great and honourable actions are accompanied with great difficulties, and must be both enterprised and overcome with answerable courages."

Six presidents of the United States had ancestors who came on the *Mayflower*. John Adams and his son John Quincy Adams were descended from John Alden and Priscilla Mullins. Zachary Taylor was descended from William Brewster and Isaac Allerton. U. S. Grant was descended from

Richard Warren, and William Howard Taft was descended from Francis Cooke.

Franklin Delano Roosevelt was descended on one side from Francis Cooke, Isaac Allerton, Richard Warren, John Howland, and John Tilley of the *Mayflower*, and on another side from Phillippe de la Noye, who came on the *Fortune* in 1621 and changed his name to Delano.

Also on the *Mayflower* came Peter Browne, whose descendant was John Brown, the famous abolitionist activist who organized and carried out the raid on Harpers Ferry, Virginia, in 1859, with the intention of capturing the United States arsenal there, arming the slaves, and bringing an end to slavery. Brown and some of his sons died in the attempt. But it was this action by him and previous actions against slavery in Missouri that alerted Americans to the evils of slavery and is widely considered the start of the Civil War.

To bring the saga of the Pilgrims full circle, one has only to read of nineteen-year-old Phillippe de la Noye, who disembarked the ship *Fortune* in early December, 1621, to announce that henceforth he would be known as Delano. And then think of his descendant, President Franklin Delano Roosevelt, who guided this country through some of its worst moments: the Depression and World War Two. And be glad that Delano and all the others decided to risk the difficulties and respond with unanswerable courage.

On September 6, 1620, 102 passengers, including 34 children, set off from Plymouth, England, aboard the Mayflower. Some of the Mayflower's passengers, known as Separatists, were going to the New World because they did not agree with the rules of the King's church. Others were going for adventure or because they could not find work in England. They were forced to leave their other ship, the Speedwell, behind because it was leaking.

After a grueling journey, the Pilgrims finally saw land on November 9, 1620. Before anyone went ashore, the Pilgrims signed the Mayflower Compact, which promised fair laws and gave the people the right to choose their own leader. They also voted that John Carver serve as governor for one year. Here, a small group of Pilgrims prepare to go ashore. The Mayflower is anchored in the distance.

After such a long trip, everyone's clothes needed to be washed. The women boiled sea water in large iron kettles on the beach of Cape Cod. The New World, unlike England, was densely forested with plenty of trees to feed the fires under the kettles.

The Pilgrims left Cape Cod in search of a better place to live. On December 16, 1620, they reached Plymouth, which Captain John Smith had named six years earlier. Despite the fields ready for planting and several sources of fresh water, the Pilgrims' first winter was a difficult one. By spring, about half of the Pilgrims were dead from a terrible illness that swept through their village.

Once the Pilgrims decided to settle in Plymouth, they worked together to build houses and the common buildings for the village.

The houses were much smaller than their homes in England, but had similar steep roofs covered with a kind of straw called thatch. Since no glass was available to make windows, the Pilgrims used oiled paper or cloth to let in some light.

In Plymouth, the Pilgrims were free to worship as they wished. These illustrations show the Pilgrims on their way to church, top, *and during church services,* bottom.

Ousamequin, or Massasoit ("Great Chief") was Grand Sachem of the Wampanoag Indians. He worked with Governor Carver on a peace treaty between the Pilgrims and the Indians. By consenting to the treaty, the Pilgrims and Indians agreed that they wouldn't attack or steal from each other. Instead, it mandated that they protect each other and leave their weapons behind when visiting each other. Although the treaty wasn't put in writing, peace lasted for fifty-four years.

149

The Pilgrims learned many things from the Indians, including where to hunt deer, turkeys, and other animals. The Indians found that they could get closer to the deer if they wore deerskins when hunting.

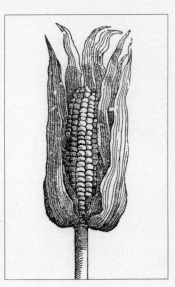

The Pilgrims found baskets of corn the first day they went ashore. Tisquantum, or Squanto, a Wampanoag of the Patuxet band who had been captured, sold into slavery, and freed by a sympathetic Englishman to return to America, taught the Pilgrims how to plant corn and use fish as fertilizer. As corn was the only crop that flourished, it probably saved their lives that first year.

150

The Pilgrims had much to be thankful for on the first Thanksgiving. They were no longer threatened by sickness, their crops were thriving, and they had become friends with the Indians. Most important, they had found a place where they could worship as they wished.

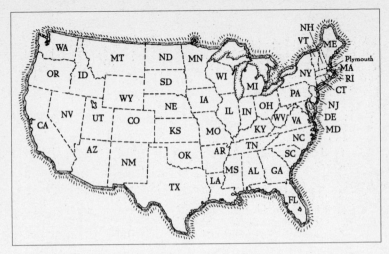

Modern map of the United States, showing the approximate location of Plymouth.

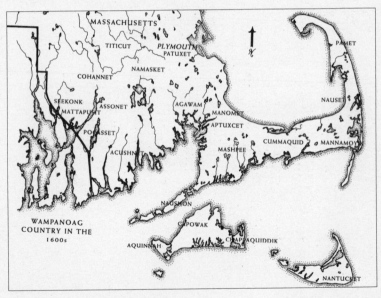

This detail of Massachusetts shows Plymouth, which the Indians called Patuxet. Also shown are nearby areas with the names used in the 1600s.

About the Author

ANN RINALDI says about writing this book, "When I first started to do research, I knew what the average American knows about the Pilgrims, that they came over on the *Mayflower*, stepped onto Plymouth Rock, and would have starved that first winter if not for help from the Indians. Then, having made it through the first year, they celebrated the first Thanksgiving.

"Once I started the research those facts became dots that needed lines to connect them and complete the picture. And the full picture is indeed a story worth pursuing.

"I was, for instance, delighted to know of the Pilgrims' life in Leyden, Holland, for a dozen or so years, and how the only reason they left was because their children were losing their English identity. I was amazed to know that the mouth of the Hudson River was considered the northernmost part of the Virginia patent they held from the king. That Elder Bradford may have left his true love back in England and that his wife, Dorothy May, may have had myriad reasons for the depression that led her to commit suicide before she set foot in the new world.

"Had anyone ever told me that Edward Dotey and Edward Leister, two indentured servants, fought America's first duel over Constance Hopkins? That Squanto, friend to the Pilgrims, had been kidnapped and sold into slavery? These and so many other 'finds' removed the Pilgrims forever for me from their static place in history and gave them flesh and blood. There is drama enough in this pivotal phase of our history to satisfy all."

Ann Rinaldi is the well-known author of numerous historical novels. She is highly regarded for her scrupulous research. Her books have been named ALA Best Books for Young Adults, CBC/IRA Young Adult Choices, and New York Public Library Books for the Teen Age. She is the author of *My Heart Is on the Ground! The Diary of Nannie Little Rose,* for the Dear America series. *Mine Eyes Have Seen* and *Second Bend in the River,* an *American Bookseller* "Pick of the Lists," are her most recent titles for Scholastic Press. She lives in Somerville, New Jersey, with her husband.

Acknowledgments

Grateful acknowledgment is made for permission to reprint the following:

Cover portrait: A detail from *Pilgrims Going to Church*, by George Henry
    Boughton, oil on canvas, 1867, accession number S-117, negative num-
ber 27117, on permanent loan from The New York Public Library.
    © Collection of The New York Historical Society.
Cover background: *The Mayflower* at sea: Colored engraving, 19th century,
    The Granger Collection.

Page 145 (top): The *Mayflower* and the *Speedwell*, courtesy of the Pilgrim
    Society, Plymouth, Massachusetts.
Page 145 (bottom): Pilgrims landing in shallop, Culver Pictures.
Page 146 (top): Laundry day, Corbis/Bettmann.
Page 146 (bottom): Pilgrims in the forest.
Page 147: Building houses, Library of Congress.
Page 148 (top): *Pilgrims Going to Church*, by George Henry Boughton,
    oil on canvas, 1867, accession number S-117, negative number 27117,
    on permanent loan from The New York Public Library. © Collection
    of The New York Historical Society.
Page 148 (bottom): Pilgrims at church.
Page 149: Winslow's visit to Massasoit, Culver Pictures.
Page 150 (top): Hunting deer.
Page 150 (bottom): Corn.
Page 151: The first Thanksgiving, courtesy of the American Museum
    of Natural History.
Page 152: Maps by Heather Saunders.

Other books in the My Name Is America series

The Journal of Ben Uchida
Citizen 13559, Mirror Lake Internment Camp
by Barry Denenberg

The Journal of William Thomas Emerson
A Revolutionary War Patriot
by Barry Denenberg

The Journal of Sean Sullivan
A Transcontinental Railroad Worker
by William Durbin

The Journal of James Edmond Pease
A Civil War Union Soldier
by Jim Murphy

The Journal of Joshua Loper
A Black Cowboy
by Walter Dean Myers

The Journal of Scott Pendleton Collins
A World War II Soldier
by Walter Dean Myers

The Journal of Wong Ming-Chung
A Chinese Miner
by Laurence Yep

For Mal and Elaine

Copyright © 2000 by Ann Rinaldi.

All rights reserved. Published by Scholastic Inc.
557 Broadway, New York, New York 10012.
MY NAME IS AMERICA®, SCHOLASTIC, and associated logos
are trademarks and/or registered trademarks of Scholastic Inc.

Library of Congress Cataloging-in-Publication Data available.

ISBN 0-590-51078-9;
ISBN 0-439-44556-6 (pbk.)

10 9 8 7 6 5 4 3 2   02 03 04 05 06

The display type was set in Deepdene.
The text type was set in Berling Roman.
Book design by Elizabeth B. Parisi
Photo research by Zoe Moffitt and Martha Davidson

Printed in the U.S.A. 23
First paperback printing, October 2002